W9-CKI-084

JF BLAIR
Blair, Kelsey, author.
Tough call

TOUGH CALL

KELSEY BLAIR

Fountaindale Public Library
Bolingbrook, IL
(630) 759-2102

James Lorimer & Company Ltd., Publishers
Toronto

Copyright © 2018 by Kelsey Blair
First published in Canada in 2018.
First published in the United States in 2020.

All rights reserved. No part of this book may be reproduced or transmitted
in any form or by any means, electronic or mechanical, including
photocopying, or by any information storage or retrieval system, without
permission in writing from the publisher.

James Lorimer & Company Ltd., Publishers acknowledges funding support
from the Ontario Arts Council (OAC), an agency of the Government
of Ontario. We acknowledge the support of the Canada Council for the
Arts, which last year invested $153 million to bring the arts to Canadians
throughout the country. This project has been made possible in part by the
Government of Canada and with the support of Ontario Creates.

Cover design: Gwen North
Cover image: Shutterstock

978-1-4594-1370-2
eBook also available 978-1-4594-1369-6

Cataloguing data available from Library and Archives Canada.

Published by:
James Lorimer &
Company Ltd., Publishers
117 Peter Street, Suite 304
Toronto, ON, Canada
M5V 0M3
www.lorimer.ca

Distributed in the US by:
Lerner Publisher Services
1251 Washington Ave. N.
Minneapolis, MN, USA
55401
www.lernerbooks.com

Printed and bound in Canada.
Manufactured by Friesens Corporation in Altona, Manitoba,
Canada in August 2019.
Job #257898

For Jim and Joan

Contents

1 A GOOD START

Malia King stares up at the basketball hoop in her middle-school gym. It's 7:45 in the morning. Her body isn't fully awake yet. She keeps her hands up, ready for the rebound. A basketball soars through the air. It clanks against the metal of the rim and falls away from the basket. Malia shifts her weight to the side. She extends her arms and catches the ball before it hits the ground.

"Ugh," says Malia's younger sister. Her name is Florence, but she goes by Flo.

"You'll make the next one." Malia passes her sister the ball. Flo shoots again. The ball hits the rim. Flo huffs loudly. "Change where you're looking."

"What?"

The ball bounces away from the hoop. Malia chases after it. "You've hit the same spot on the rim twice in a row. Change your target by looking someplace else." Malia picks up the ball and passes it to Flo.

Flo shoots. This time, the ball falls through the mesh of the hoop. "It worked," she says.

"Of course it worked," says Malia, teasing her sister. "I said it. Your turn to rebound."

The sisters switch places. Malia holds up her hands, signalling to Flo to throw her the ball. Her sister passes it to her, and Malia shoots. As the ball falls through the basket, a burst of energy surges through Malia's body.

That, thinks Malia, *is a good way to start the day*.

Malia moves to another spot and gets ready to shoot. "How are you feeling about tryouts later?"

"Bad," replies Flo.

"That's dramatic."

"It's not," says Flo, her voice shaking a bit. "I've never tried out for a basketball team before. In lower grades, everyone just made the team. What if I'm not good enough?"

"You are good enough."

"We'll see."

Malia catches the ball, but she doesn't shoot. Instead she walks toward the hoop.

"What are you doing?" Flo asks.

"You can shoot again. Get some extra reps before tryouts."

"But you're not done your turn."

"I'll live." Malia passes her sister the ball. "Go on."

Flo takes Malia's place. The girls keep shooting until the bell rings.

***

Malia bounces her leg up and down in French class. The movement makes her desk shake, but Malia doesn't care. She looks up at the clock. There are two minutes left until the lunch bell, and the first meeting of the season for her grade nine girls' basketball team. She glances down at her textbook. It's filled with homework questions she could be answering. She looks up at the clock: one minute and forty-three seconds left.

When the bell sounds, Malia hops up from her desk. She grabs her textbook, throws it in her backpack and slings the bag over her shoulder. Even though she sits five desks away from the door, she is the first person out of the classroom and into the hall. The second is her best friend, Priya. Priya holds her lunch bag in one hand, her phone in the other and an apple between her teeth.

"Here," says Malia, reaching out to Priya. "I can carry your lunch."

"Thanks," mumbles Priya through her apple. She hands over the lunch bag and stares intensely at her phone as the two girls weave through the crowded hallways of Vancouver East Side Middle School. Priya takes a big bite of her apple, then grabs it with her free hand. "How long do you think the basketball meeting is going to be?" she asks.

"No clue. Why?"

"I've got to pick up an early dismissal slip. I have a cross-country meet this afternoon."

"Don't you have soccer today?"

"Yup. But it isn't until later." Priya frowns at her phone again. "This meeting is probably just the season's schedule and a breakdown of the fees."

Malia winces at the word 'fees.' She hates that basketball costs her parents money.

"That shouldn't take too long, right?" Priya asks. She doesn't notice Malia's reaction.

The girls walk into the gym. Their coach, Lucy Cruz, stands on the court with a woman Malia doesn't know. Their teammates Zoe and Valentina sit in front of the women, chatting. Priya and Malia join them and, in minutes, the rest of the players arrive in the gym.

"Welcome to our first basketball meeting of the season," says Coach Lucy brightly. She passes a stack of papers to each player. "Please, please, please. Try not to lose these before you get home tonight. This package contains key information about our season this year. It includes our game schedule, our tournament schedule, team expectations, parent expectations and —"

"There are expectations for our parents?" asks Zoe.

Coach Lucy purses her lips together. When she opens her mouth, she speaks each word as if it is part of a pre-game speech: clear, firm and with intent. "After the incident during the playoffs between East Side and Boundary Middle School, both schools felt they had to implement expectations for parental behaviour."

"You mean because Todd's dad got in a fight with

one of the crazy Boundary parents?" asks Zoe.

"It wasn't a fight. It was an argument," replies Coach Lucy.

"I was there. They were screaming at each other."

"Sometimes people scream in arguments. The point is that now both schools have parental expectations." Coach Lucy flips open to the right page and points at a line on the bottom of it. "To prove that your parents have read this, I need them to sign the form and return it to me."

Zoe raises her hand again, but Coach Lucy waves her off. "Don't worry. I've sent an email to your parents telling them what to do. This," she says, pointing at the package, "is just so that they have a paper copy. It also has a full listing of all the fees for the year. Any questions?" All the girls shake their heads. "Good. Before I let you go, I want to introduce you to Gloria Rieve. She's the head of the Vancouver Basketball Referee Association, and she's here to share some information with us."

Malia looks at Gloria, who is wearing high-heeled shoes and a pencil skirt. She looks more like a business woman than a ref. Glancing down at her own jeans and purple hooded sweatshirt, Malia realizes she probably looks more like a regular teenager than a basketball player.

"Look, girls," says Gloria. "I know that when you started playing basketball, none of you dreamed of being a referee. But in games, we're as important as the ball, the hoops, the coaches and even the players. And we're looking to recruit new members . . ."

Malia's mind drifts as Gloria talks. Gloria's right. Malia has never considered being a ref. All they do is point out players' mistakes and get yelled at by coaches. Why would anyone sign up for that?

"It's also a good way to make some extra money." These words catch Malia's attention. "Referees get paid per game, and it is well above minimum wage."

"Really?" asks Zoe.

"Really," confirms Gloria.

"Think about whether you are interested in taking the course and getting certified," continues Gloria. "I'm going to leave a sign-up sheet outside the gym office."

2 The DECISION

Priya strides out of the office. "Lunch is a success," she declares. She holds up her pink early dismissal slip.

"I don't know that a dismissal slip is enough to make lunch successful," says Malia with doubt in her voice.

"Sure it is," replies Priya. "I forgot to get my slip last week, and I couldn't leave last block. I was almost late for the cross-country meet. But not this week!"

"You're right," says Malia, high fiving Priya. "That is a success."

The pair walk down the hallway toward the cafeteria. "I'm stoked for basketball this year," says Malia. "Think we can beat Boundary?"

Priya knits her eyebrows together, thinking about it. "Yes," she says finally. "We're going to have to work for it. Their shooting guard is the real deal."

"No kidding," agrees Malia. "She scored twenty-five points against us last year. And their tall girl . . ."

"Number 20, I think?"

"She's good, too."

Priya nods. "But we're the stronger team. You, me and Lindsay can take turns dealing with the shooting guard. And Valentina can handle Number 20. And all of us can score. We've just got to come together."

As the girls enter the cafeteria, Malia asks, "What did you think about the whole reffing thing?"

Priya shrugs. "I didn't, really. I barely have time to do my homework as it is."

"Right."

"You?"

Before Malia can answer, the girls reach the table where their friends sit. Victor Liu looks right at Malia. "Hey," he says smoothly.

Malia feels a warmth rise in her cheeks. "Hi," she squeaks out.

Priya smirks. She knows Malia has had a crush on Victor since the beginning of the year. Malia steals a quick glance. She's not sure what it is about Victor that makes her blush. He's taller than she is, but not by much. His black hair is always brushed. It perfectly frames his oval face and brown eyes. But there is no one thing that makes him stand out.

It must be all of those things together, thinks Malia.

As usual, their friends are in the middle of a discussion about the morning classes. Sean, Victor's best friend, complains about math class. Zoe laughs at everything Sean says. Everyone shuffles over on the bench to make room for Malia and Priya. Just as Malia is about to slide into her spot, she notices Flo at the edge of the cafeteria.

Priya follows Malia's gaze. "Why is Flo just standing there?" she asks Malia.

"No idea." Flo signals for Malia to come talk to her. Malia waves back, inviting Flo to her table. Flo shakes her head. "My sister is so weird."

"Mine's weirder."

"That's true," says Malia playfully. Malia gets up from the table. "I'll go see what's up."

"You can come into the cafeteria, you know," Malia says as she gets near Flo.

Flo shakes her head. "It's where the grade nines eat."

"We don't bite."

"Your friends don't." She looks around suspiciously. "Can't be sure about the rest."

Malia rolls her eyes. "Why are you here then?"

"I forgot my lunch," Flo mumbles.

"Are your friends not sharing theirs with you?" asks Malia firmly. "Because I might bite them if —"

"No," says Flo quickly. "They did. But I've got basketball tryouts after school. And I'm going to be hungry and distracted the whole time. And none of it matters anyway. Because even if I make the team, I probably can't play."

"Why not?"

"The fee," says Flo. "What if Mom and Dad can't pay for both of us?"

Malia looks at her little sister. The day before, Flo was shouting at Malia through the bathroom door for taking too long in the shower. Now she's standing in front of Malia, her bottom lip quivering with emotion. "They would have told you they couldn't afford the fee before you tried out for the team."

"Maybe," says Flo. "Or maybe they think I won't make it, so they don't have to worry about it."

"Flo," says Malia seriously, "you were the leading scorer on your school team last year, and you've been putting your work in. So you're ready." Her sister raises an eyebrow. "We shot around this morning and you did great."

"That's true."

"So if you go out there and play your hardest, you'll make the team."

Flo sighs.

When Malia tried out for her first middle-school team, she was so nervous she couldn't eat. But she would never tell her sister that. "Come on," she says. She grabs Flo's wrist and tugs her into the cafeteria. "Let's get you some food for later."

Malia drags Flo to the table where her friends sit. They all wave at her, but Flo's eyes dart around nervously. Malia grabs her backpack.

"Where are you going?" asks Priya.

"Going to get Flo something to eat. And then I have to go do something. I'll see you in English."

The Decision

Malia guides Flo through the cafeteria line. She picks up a ham and cheese sandwich and an apple. "Will this work?"

Flo nods, and Malia goes to the cashier.

"I'll pay you back," says Flo.

Malia shakes her head. "Don't worry about it. I baby-sit, so I have some money." She hands Flo the food.

"Thanks," mumbles Flo. She begins to shuffle out of the cafeteria.

"Flo," Malia calls to her sister, who turns back. "Not that you'll need it, but good luck this afternoon."

Flo nods seriously. Malia watches her sister leave the cafeteria. She's sure what she said to Flo was true. Her parents wouldn't let both girls try out for basketball if they couldn't afford to pay the fees. Malia glances at her friends. Priya plays 800 sports and never thinks twice about how much they cost. But Malia's parents don't work in fancy offices like Priya's do. Malia tucks the change from Flo's food into her pocket. Babysitting money is good for things like buying candy at the corner store or going to the movies. But Malia doesn't make nearly enough to help her parents with the cost of basketball.

Malia looks at the clock on the wall. Five minutes until afternoon classes. *Just enough time*, thinks Malia.

She strides out of the cafeteria, pumping her arms like she's competing in a speed-walking race. She dodges a gaggle of grade eight girls giggling as they

17

walk. She steps over a chess game being played in the middle of the hallway. She scurries past a grade seven cheerleading practice. When she reaches the phys ed office door, she grabs a pen and signs up for the reffing course.

3 TRAINING BEGINS

"There she is," says their mom proudly as Flo walks onto the court in her first grade seven exhibition game. "Oh! She'll be so pleased to be starting the game."

"Of course she's starting," replies Malia. "She's good."

"Have you told her that?" asks her mom with a raised eyebrow.

"I have, actually."

On the court, the players gather at centre. Flo stands outside the jump-ball circle beside her teammate Tilda, who is Victor's sister. The two exchange a serious glance as the ref walks to the centre of the court with the ball. Malia tries to see herself in the striped shirt, a whistle around her neck. It's far easier to see herself wearing one of the player's uniforms. But maybe that will change by the end of the day.

"Go Ducks!" cheers Malia's mom.

"Mom."

"What? That's the name of your school team isn't it?"

"It is, but . . ."

"No buts. I don't get to see the two of you play enough." She takes a deep breath and yells loudly, "Go Ducks!"

On the court, the ref tosses the ball into the air. The two players in the jump-ball circle leap for it. The East Side player gets there first and taps the ball to her teammate. The game begins.

Malia watches Flo and her friends run up and down the court. They're not as skilled as Malia's grade nine teammates. But the players' energy is no different. Everyone is trying their hardest. Flo moves around the court like a lion stalking its prey. Each move is intentional, fast and fierce. The third time down the court, Flo receives the ball on the wing, a spot outside the three-point line. She fakes a shot, and her defender bounds into the air to try to block her. Flo easily dodges the contact. She speeds past the defender toward the hoop. By the time the other players on the court can react, Flo is near the basket. She shoots. The ball flies through the air, hits the backboard and goes through the orange rim.

"You go, Flo!" cheers Malia's mom.

"Mom," chides Malia.

"Your sister scored. We must cheer."

"Yeah. But maybe don't rhyme when you do it."

"So I should stop rhyming when I cheer for you then?"

Training Begins

"Oh my God," says Malia, a tightness filling her chest. "You don't actually do that, do you?"

Her mom laughs. "It's much harder to find something that rhymes with Malia. But I bet I could manage it if you really want me to." She winks, and then looks up at the clock. "Shouldn't you get going to your course?"

"I've seen exactly three minutes of the game."

"There will be other games. And you don't want to be late."

"I guess not."

Even though she doesn't want to, Malia gets up. She walks to the top of the bleachers and looks down at the game. Flo is still zipping around the court. She looks like she might die if her team doesn't get every defensive rebound. Malia wishes she could stay. She looks up at the clock. Her mom is right. It's time to go.

Malia strides out of the school and down the twelve blocks to the reffing course. When she gets to the community centre, Malia follows hand-made paper signs that direct her to a small room at the back. Malia pushes through the room's grey door. Right away, she notices two things. First, there isn't a basketball in sight. Second, she doesn't know anyone.

Malia looks around. Gloria stands at the front of the room. She has a whistle around her neck, a pen behind her ear and a clipboard in her hand. A cluster of men — who look like they might be part of a seniors' lawn bowling team — stand together and chat loudly. In the

21

corner, older teenagers, wearing hoodies from their high schools, lean against a wall and try to look cool.

Malia sits down in one of the chairs at the back. A boy with long legs sits two chairs down. Even though his height takes up a lot of space, he seems to be the same age as Malia.

Gloria claps. "All right. Everyone take a seat. We're going to get started."

Everyone finds a seat. Gloria walks to the corner of the room and picks up a stack of thick manuals. She passes them around the room.

"As this is a refereeing course, the rules of the game are, clearly, very important," she says. "In this manual, you'll find a complete, updated list of the rules of basketball. But equally important, if not even more so than the rules, are the people. Refs always work in partners. At higher levels, you might even work in a trio. So I'd like to start today by having each of you introduce yourself to someone you don't know. Tell them who you are, where you're from and what brought you here."

Malia looks around. She makes eye contact with the tall boy. "Hi."

"Hey," he replies. "I'm Carlos."

"Malia."

"I go to Boundary."

"Middle school?" asks Malia. Her tone is harsher than she intended, but how could it not be? The rich kids from Boundary can't be trusted. Everyone knows that. Well, everyone at East Side knows it. "I go to East Side."

"Cool. What's the other thing we're supposed to say?"

"Why we're here."

"Oh," he says. Malia thinks he looks a little nervous. "I like basketball. I watch it all the time with my mom. And I'm tall so everyone thinks that I should play. Until they actually see me play," he says with a chuckle. "Then they don't think that anymore. I thought it'd be cool to be part of the game in a different way. You?"

Malia hesitates. She's not going to tell some random Boundary kid that she's here because she needs the money. "I play. Thought it'd be good to learn more about the game."

"Nice," he says warmly. His eyes flicker to the front of the room where the high-school kids sit. "I think we're the youngest people here."

Malia looks around. "Yeah. Seems that way."

"All right!" says Gloria from the front of the room. "Now that we've all made a friend, let's get going. Everyone open your manual to the first page."

Malia turns the page of her manual. It's like a textbook. Every page is packed with words.

***

Five hours and a lunch break later, Gloria is explaining a key concept. "You have to remember that players have the right to the space directly above their heads and below their feet."

"Below their feet?" asks one of the older men at the front. "I thought the game was played on the court, not beneath it."

He looks around to get laughs from his pals. Gloria grits her teeth in a half smiling, half annoyed jaw clench. "The space below their feet refers to when a player jumps. Even when they're in the air, a player has the right to land where they took off."

That gets Malia's interest. "What if a player doesn't land where they take off?"

"Great question!" says Gloria. "If there is no one else in the space the player jumps into, then that's fine. If that's not the case, things get complicated. Let's say an offensive player jumps to take a shot, runs into a defensive player who is standing still and knocks them down. In this case, it would be the offensive player's foul. But . . ." says Gloria. She uses her fingers to show what she means. "If the offensive player and the defensive player are both moving, then it could be either player's foul. That is where a ref needs to make a judgement call. And all calls, as you'll soon find out, happen very quickly. It isn't thought. It's instinct."

"Cool," says Malia under her breath.

Gloria looks down at her watch. "I think that's enough for today."

"Thank God," whispers Gina, one of the teenage

by a player wearing a yellow jersey. The defender is aggressive, crowding the offensive player's space. But the defensive player doesn't make illegal contact. To get away from the defender, the offensive player makes a move to the basket. Before bouncing the ball, she shuffles her feet. When a player moves their feet before bouncing the ball, it breaks the travelling rule. Malia knows this, but she hesitates before making the call.

What if she saw it wrong?

The offensive player bursts past the defensive player and scores a basket.

"That was a travel," complains the defensive player.

Malia can't answer. The next action sequence has already begun.

A yellow player dribbles the ball up the court. She's fast and the blue team is caught off guard. The player with the ball blasts toward the hoop. A blue player sprints ahead of her. Rather than trying to cut her off, the defensive player plants herself in front of the hoop, directly in the offensive player's path. The player with the ball looks up. She sees the defensive player standing completely still in front of her, but she doesn't stop. The two players collide. The defensive player falls backward, the offensive player tumbling on top of her.

Malia blows her whistle. "Charge!" she says, making the signal for the foul at the same time.

The offensive player hops to her feet. "What?!" she demands. "She tripped me."

"Because you ran into her," replies Malia quietly.

Gloria blows her whistle three times, signalling the end of the mock game. She turns to the offensive player. "Malia's right. That was an offensive call. Refs! Gather round!" The refs jog to Gloria. "That was a great session," she says. "One thing I'm noticing though, is that some of you are making calls that are out of your zone. Gina," she says, pointing at one of the teenage girls. "What's a zone?"

"A kind of defence?"

"Incorrect. Murray?" Gloria says, pointing at one of the older men.

"The area of the court each referee is responsible for."

"That's right. And while it isn't illegal to make calls out of your zone, it's not good practice to do so. You should be paying attention to other areas. Something for you all to think about before next week!" Everyone nods. "Malia, can I talk to you for a second?"

Gloria pulls Malia to the side of the gym. "The charging call you made at the end of the scrimmage was a good one."

"Thanks."

"You understand the game and have good instincts. But you need to be more assertive. Basketball is a fast game. It's dynamic. You need to trust those instincts. Will you make mistakes? Sometimes. But you'll make a lot less mistakes than players, coaches or fans accuse you of. Trust yourself to make the right call."

"Okay," says Malia. "Thanks."

"Now go get some water. You've earned it."

Malia walks to the side of the court. People slowly make their way out of the gym. Carlos hands Malia her water bottle, and she takes a big gulp. "How'd your game go?" he asks.

"Okay," says Malia. "I missed a travel call."

"That's nothing. I missed three fouls. In the same offensive possession." Carlos runs his long fingers through his thick brown hair. "It's just a rec game. But I thought the players were going to murder me."

"I'm sure it wasn't that bad."

"Gloria had to stop the game to calm everyone down. I think I'm actually worse at reffing than I am at playing."

"Impossible," says Malia, nudging him playfully.

"Hey!" he says, a smile on his lips. "You've never even seen me play."

"I wouldn't have said that if I had," counters Malia. "I bet you're decent at basketball. You're too tall not to be."

"I can't catch."

"As a ref, people pass you the ball all the time. You haven't dropped it once."

"I don't know if that counts."

Malia picks up a nearby basketball. She bounce-passes it to Carlos, and he easily catches it. "See," she says, tilting her head to the side. "You can catch."

Malia signals that she wants the ball, and Carlos passes it to her. Malia walks onto the empty court toward one of the baskets. Carlos follows.

"Do you want to know what I think?" she says.

"If I say no, will that stop you?" he asks teasingly.

"I think you're too hard on yourself. So you missed some calls. You'll do better next time."

Malia spins the ball in her hand a couple times. The leather rubs against her palm. She looks at the basket and moves into shooting position, feet shoulder-width apart, elbow bent. She shoots and watches as the ball flies through the air toward the rim. The empty gym is quiet. So when the ball falls through the mesh netting of the basket, Malia hears a gentle *swoosh*. As much as Malia enjoys reffing, it's hard to beat the feeling of scoring a basket.

Carlos chases after the ball. He picks it up and passes it back to Malia. Then he stands under the hoop to rebound for her.

"I think the hardest part of reffing is the speed," says Carlos as Malia takes another shot. "Everything happens so fast when you're in it, you know? When I watch games on TV, it's easy to see when a ref misses a call or gets something wrong. But when it's you making the calls, it's a whole other game."

"Tell me about it," says Malia, thinking about her own mistake. She glances at the clock in the corner of the gym. "Ack!"

"What?"

"I've got practice in twenty minutes."

"On a Saturday night?"

"Between Priya's soccer practices and Julia's piano lessons, it's hard to find time everyone can be at practice. And with regular season coming up, we've got to work on team principles. Not that I should be telling a Boundary boy our team's secrets."

"Oh, yeah," says Carlos, rolling his eyes. "Because the grade nine girls' basketball team cares what I think."

"They should," says Malia. "You know what you're talking about. See you next week!"

5 FOULS

Malia runs into the gym just before practice starts. She swings her backpack off her shoulder. She rummages through the reffing gear, searching for her basketball shoes.

"Hey," says Zoe. She plops down beside Malia to put on her own shoes. As she sits, her eyes wander to Malia's bag. "How's reffing going?"

"I like it, actually. It's interesting."

"Really?"

"Yeah. This week, Gloria went over the vertical plane principle again."

"That sounds *super* interesting," says Zoe with an eye roll.

"It's one of the core ideas of the game," says Malia defensively. She remembers Gloria standing at the front of the room, explaining the concept. "Every player has a right to the space they're already standing in. It means that no one can tackle you when you have the ball. That space is called a player's cylinder."

Fouls

"Hm," says Zoe thoughtfully.

Coach Lucy blows the whistle to signal the start of practice. Malia yanks her shoes from the very bottom of her bag and rushes to put them on.

"Let's go, girls!" says Coach Lucy.

Malia hops down the bleachers, wearing a sock on one foot and a basketball shoe on the other. She laces up her second shoe as Coach Lucy talks.

"Today, we're going to work on team defence. If we want to be successful this season and beat the really good teams —"

"Like Boundary," interjects Zoe.

"They aren't the only good team. But yes, teams like Boundary. We have to make people uncomfortable on offence. We do that through assertive team defence. To practice, we're going to start with some pressure layups. I want two lines on the baseline."

The team follows Coach Lucy's instructions. She passes basketballs to the first three girls in the line furthest from the basket. She walks ten paces and places a cone on the court in front of the line. "This is the offensive line. When I blow the whistle, you will dribble the ball around the cone. Then make a full-speed move toward the basket to shoot a layup."

She takes one pace backward and places a cone in front of the other line. "This is the defensive line. When I blow the whistle, you will run around the cone and try to challenge the offensive player's layup.

The goal is to put pressure on every shot. Are we clear?"

Malia and her teammates nod.

Zoe is the first player in the defensive line, and Priya is the first player in the offensive line. Coach Lucy blows the whistle, and the girls sprint toward the cones. They both go around their cones at the same time, sprinting toward the basket. Priya raises her arm to shoot. Zoe jumps, swinging her arm to swat the ball. Zoe misses and clearly touches Priya's wrist. The contact makes Priya miss the shot.

"Good hustle, Zoe," says Coach Lucy.

When Malia gets to the front of the defensive line, she's paired with Penelope. The whistle blows and Malia sprints toward her cone. When she gets to the cone, she plants her foot and quickly pivots to change direction. Penelope bobbles the ball as she dribbles. Malia catches her and swings at the ball. Like Zoe, Malia hits the ball and Penelope's wrist. Penelope misses the shot.

"Good, Malia."

Except, thinks Malia, *I fouled Penelope. Shouldn't we be learning to play defence without fouling?*

After practice, Malia sits down next to Priya to untie her shoes. "Do you think Coach Lucy should have let those fouls go in that layup drill?" she asks.

"You're over-thinking it," says Priya. "Coach Lucy is just encouraging us to be aggressive."

"She didn't say aggressive. She said assertive."

"They're pretty close."

"But they aren't the same. Or . . . I don't think they are."

"Well, don't worry about it too much. We'll rein in our defence when we have to."

"Will we be able to?"

"Of course we will," says Priya confidently. "Besides, who says the ref will call the fouls?"

"Any ref would call those fouls. Even Carlos."

"That's your reffing friend? The one from Boundary?"

"It is."

"Right," says Priya coldly.

"Right, what?"

She shrugs. "I don't know. Do you really want to be hanging out with someone from Boundary?"

"I'm not hanging out with him." Malia hesitates. "Well, I am. But we're the youngest people there and . . ." Malia is caught off guard by finding herself saying good things about Carlos. "He's nice."

"So you're defending him?"

"I'm not defending anyone. Because no one's done anything wrong. He just goes to another school."

"Our rival school." Priya stares at Malia with steely eyes.

Malia would have said the exact same thing four weeks ago. But she wouldn't say it now. Not about Carlos. She shakes the confusing thoughts out of her head. "My point was that any ref, even a new one, would call fouls on us."

Priya relents. "Fine. Maybe they would. But I think it's good we're learning to be aggressive."

"I do, too. I just . . ." Malia sighs. Maybe Priya is right. Maybe she's over-thinking it. "I don't want anything to stop us from winning."

Priya's phone buzzes. She looks at the screen and lets out a long sigh.

"Everything okay?" Malia asks.

"My soccer coach just moved practice time on Monday."

"Why?"

"Something about a double-booking on the field. But I have cross-country practice at the same time as the new soccer practice."

"Oh. That sucks."

"It's just . . . annoying," says Priya. She runs her hands through her hair. "I don't want to miss soccer. We're working on this new short corner play. It's got all these different parts, and we're going to be so hard to stop if we can do it properly."

"Cool."

"But I like cross country. And I've committed to that team, too."

"Could you go split the practices?" suggests Malia. "Go to the first half of cross country and the second half of soccer?"

"I would have to get from one to the other. But

I guess?" Priya zips up her bag. "I'll deal with it later. Want to get dinner?"

"Yes!" says Malia. "I'm so hungry I could eat two dinners."

6 JUDGEMENT CALLS

Carlos and Malia sit together at the back of the meeting room. They stare at a small TV set, wheeled to the front of the room by Gloria. An old basketball game flickers on the screen in front of them. It's the fourth quarter of a close game. Even on the small screen, the players' emotions are visible. Malia's heart beats a little faster, watching as the ball flies up and down the court.

An offensive player, wearing the brightest yellow jersey Malia has ever seen, has the ball. He glances off-screen, probably up at the play clock. He passes to a teammate who is running up the sideline, looking over his shoulder. What his teammate doesn't see is that the defensive player, wearing a much saner-coloured green jersey, anticipates the pass. The defender jumps into the offensive player's path. As the offensive player grabs the ball, the two bodies collide. Everything is a jumble of green, yellow and limbs.

Gloria pauses the game. She looks out at the room. "So what call would you make?"

Gina raises her hand. "It's a blocking foul. No doubt."

"Why?"

"The dude in green ran the other guy over. What is there to explain?"

"In the language of referees, please," says Gloria sternly.

Gina huffs. "There was illegal contact. The defender ran into the offensive player, so it's his foul."

"The defensive player wasn't moving when they hit," argues Murray. "I think it's a charge."

"Why?" asks Gloria.

"It's what you said about the cylinder the first day," says Murray. "The defensive player has a right to their space. He moved to get into that space, but his feet were set when they hit. That's a charging foul on the offence."

"His feet weren't set," argues Gina.

"Let's see it again."

"No can do," says Gloria. "In the pro leagues, they can sometimes look at video. But at this level, you never get to see things twice. You must decide. And sometimes it's not obvious what that decision should be. This is the final lesson in our course: judgement calls."

"That's not in the manual," says Murray.

"It's not," says Gloria with a nod. "Did you know that when basketball was first invented, the game only had thirteen rules?" Everyone stares at Gloria, intrigued. "Now rulebooks are dozens of pages long.

The people who write those rules want to be clear. They detail what to do in a range of situations. Don't get me wrong, that's really helpful to you as a ref. You need to know the rules of the game like you know the route from your bedroom to your bathroom — well enough that you could call a game half-asleep. But the rulebook doesn't have all the answers. Sometimes you need to make a judgement call based on your experience of a situation. Crucially, you need to trust your experience and your judgement." She points at the TV. "Because in close games, half the people in the gym are going to be mad at you no matter what you do."

"That sucks," says Gina.

"You get used to it," says Gloria with a wink. She grabs a stack of papers from the table beside her. "It's been an absolute pleasure teaching you all. Based on the information you gave me last week about your availability, I've got a schedule for each of you. I have made this schedule based on several factors, including your own schedule, your experience level and your age. Except for illness or emergencies, I can't make any switches. If any of you cancels last minute or fails to show up for a game, I will take you out of the rotation," she says seriously. "In addition to being fun, remember that refereeing is also a job."

That's right, thinks Malia, *money!*

Gloria hands out the schedules. "Carlos and Malia, I'd like to speak with you both."

"Have we done something wrong?" whispers Carlos.

"Don't know," replies Malia nervously.

Gloria hands them both a piece of paper. "As the youngest people in the course, neither of you can drive to games. And I don't want you reffing people older than you. So I've scheduled you both to ref several grade seven and eight games that involve your middle school teams."

"Is that bad?" asks Carlos.

"Not at all. But I understand why that could be a little complicated. So for those games, I've paired you with the same partner each time to add some consistency. Carlos, you'll be reffing with Murray. Malia, you'll be reffing with Gina."

Malia and Carlos nod. Gloria hands them their sheets before crossing the room to talk to Murray.

Malia looks down at her sheet. She furrows her brow.

"You okay?" asks Carlos.

"Yeah, it's just . . . I'm scheduled to work a bunch of my little sister's games."

"Oh."

"Yeah," says Malia. "That's how I feel. 'Oh.'" She glances over at Gloria, who is chatting with a very excited Murray. "But I don't want to lose half my work."

"If it helps," says Carlos. "You're a really good ref. Your sister should be happy to have you."

"I have a funny feeling she won't feel that way," says Malia. She taps her foot on the ground. "But you know what? She's just going to have to get over it. She's part of the reason I took the course in the first place."

"Hm?"

Malia thinks it would be nice to share the real reason she's reffing with someone. "It's . . ." Malia notices the thick block letters of Carlos's Boundary Middle School sweatshirt, ". . . a long story. I'll tell you another time."

"Cool," he says with a shrug. "Want to grab pizza? I'm starving."

"Uh . . ." Pizza costs money. This isn't how Malia wants to be spending her money. She looks at Carlos who is waiting for her answer. His expression is kind and hopeful. "We should celebrate finishing the course," she decides. "Let's do it."

"Nice!"

7 LATE CALLS

Malia stands to the side of the basketball court. She watches two teams of grade-seven girls warm up. She holds her hands out in front of her. They tremble with nerves.

"Ready?"

Malia turns and looks up to see Carlos towering above her. "Hey." She tilts her head to the side. "Why are you here?"

"It's your first game," says Carlos simply. "How are you feeling?"

"Terrified. What if I screw up?"

"You won't."

"But what if I do?"

"Then you'll move on to the next play. Like Gloria said." He looks around the gym. "Where's your partner?"

Malia nods at the scorekeepers' table. Gina leans back in her chair, her feet on the table and gobbles a sandwich.

Carlos knits his eyebrows together. "Do high-school kids like her?"

"I think so. The ones in our course seemed to."

43

Gina loses her balance, falling backward out of her chair. Eyes wide, she hops to her feet and looks around. Thinking no one noticed, she pretends to brush off her uniform.

"I don't understand the world," says Carlos, watching Gina.

Malia smiles. She looks up at the clock. "I better get ready."

"Good luck!"

Malia walks up to Gina. "Hey."

"Yo."

"We're working together today."

"I figured that," says Gina with a wink. There's something about the wink that Malia is unsure of. "I'm going to toss the jump ball."

"Okay."

Gina and Malia introduce themselves to the coaches. The horn sounds to signal a minute left before the game starts. Malia takes her position. The players from both teams — the Almond Grove Wild Cats and the Bayshore Owls — gather at centre court. Gina tosses the ball into the air. Her throw goes off-kilter and favours the Wild Cats, but Gina allows play to continue.

"That was brutal," says the Owls' coach.

Malia looks at him and nods. But she doesn't say anything. It isn't her place to correct Gina's mistakes. Or is it?

Malia refocuses her attention on the game. A Wild

Cats player catches the ball on the wing. She takes a step without dribbling the ball.

Malia blows her whistle to stop play, but she doesn't put enough force into it. No one hears the sound.

"Travel!" yells the Owls' coach.

The player takes another step. Malia blows her whistle again. The play stops. "Travel," says Malia quietly. She makes the travelling gesture. It feels like everyone in the gym is annoyed with her. The feeling makes Malia's stomach twist into a knot.

The knot gets tighter as the game goes on. Malia sees fouls but it seems like she's always a half second too late. And when she does blow her whistle, it's never quite loud enough. When the horn finally sounds to signal the end of the game, Malia stomps to the score-keepers' table, frustrated with herself.

"That went well," says Gina. She takes a gulp of her water bottle.

"Seriously? We missed a million calls."

"It's a grade-seven game," she says dismissively. "It's fine."

Malia's eyes go wide. Her instinct is to reach for Gina's water bottle and to squirt water in her face. But she stops herself and backs away from the scorekeepers' table.

She sees Carlos in the stands and goes to join him. "Gina is the worst," Malia tells him.

"She's not the world's best ref."

"Not that. Well, that, too. But it's more that she doesn't care because it's a grade-seven game. I know they're younger, but grade sevens are people, too." Malia lets out a long, slow exhale.

"That's a big sigh," says Carlos.

"That was awful. I was awful."

"Awful is pretty harsh."

Malia raises her eyebrow.

"It wasn't awful." Then Carlos relents. "But I've seen you be more . . . assertive?"

"I second-guessed everything."

"You shouldn't do that."

"No kidding."

"Really, though," says Carlos. "Gina never thinks twice, and she's half the ref you are. Next time, trust yourself. I do."

"Thanks," says Malia. "I have to get to my own practice. But I'll come watch your first game tomorrow."

"You don't have to do that," says Carlos. His cheeks redden slightly.

"It's true. I don't. I'll still see you tomorrow," she adds with a smile.

★★★

"All right, ladies," says Coach Lucy. "Water break is over."

Malia takes one last gulp of water before jogging

toward Coach Lucy.

"We're going to finish today's practice with chase layups."

The players line up on the baseline. Coach Lucy places a cone in front of each line. Malia is at the front of the offensive line. Priya is at the front of the defensive line.

"Ready?" asks Coach Lucy.

Priya winks at Malia. "Bring it."

"Born ready," replies Malia, smiling.

Coach Lucy blows the whistle, and both Malia and Priya sprint toward their cones. Malia dribbles the ball as she runs. When she gets to her cone, she crosses the ball from her right hand to her left hand and then back again. She turns and explodes toward the basket. She can hear Priya's feet pounding the court as she chases Malia. Malia keeps her eyes focused on the rim. She feels the heat of Priya's body beside her. Suddenly, Priya reaches for the ball, but Malia moves her body so that it protects the ball. As Malia shoots, Priya accidentally slaps Malia's shoulder. But it doesn't matter. Malia's shot falls through the net of the hoop.

"Nice finish, Malia," encourages Zoe from the baseline.

"Good offence and good defence."

In a game, thinks Malia, *Priya would get called for a foul. But this is practice. So maybe that doesn't matter?*

Coach Lucy blows the whistle and Zoe and Lauren

race toward their cones. Lauren, the offensive player, gets to her cone before Zoe gets to hers. The two sprint toward the basket but Zoe doesn't really have a chance. As Lauren jumps into the air, Zoe reaches out. She aims for the ball but contacts Lauren's arm.

"Foul!" cries Lauren.

"If there's no call, there's no foul," replies Zoe with a shrug.

"That's not true," says Malia before she can stop herself.

Zoe's eyes narrow with anger at Malia. She opens her mouth to retort, but Coach Lucy cuts her off. "It was a foul. We want to be aggressive, but within the rules." She glances at Malia. "And some of us might be a little more aware of fouls now that we're reffing."

"No kidding," mumbles Zoe.

Malia looks around. Her teammates nod, silently agreeing with Coach Lucy. The knot in Malia's stomach tightens again. Malia tries to shake it away and focus on the next play.

8 GAME CHANGER

Malia adjusts the front of her ref uniform. Then she walks to the scorekeepers' table to introduce herself. In the month since her first game, she's learned that connecting with scorekeepers is key to a smooth game.

"Hey," says Malia to two girls sitting behind the score clock. "I'm Malia."

"Anna."

"Maria."

"Nice to meet you both. Have you done this before?"

The girls nod.

"Do you have any questions about how to run the clock?"

They shake their heads.

"Or anything else?"

"Is she in high school?" asks Anna. Her voice is high with excitement, as she nods to Gina.

"She is."

The girls giggle.

"I wouldn't get too excited," Malia cautions them.

The horn sounds, signalling a minute before the game begins. Gina joins Malia. "Shall we?"

Malia nods. They walk over to the home-team bench. Gina reaches out her hand to introduce herself to East Side's coach. The coach takes it and shakes it vigorously.

"I'm —" Gina starts.

"Gina," says the coach. "You went to East Side, didn't you?"

Gina nods and smiles proudly.

The coach looks at Malia. "And you I know."

Malia nods and holds out her hand. During the day, she is the music teacher at East Side. But right now she's a coach.

Malia and Gina walk over to the Boundary bench and introduce themselves.

Gina moves to the score table. She reaches for the ball so she can throw the toss for the jump ball.

Malia rushes over and quickly picks it up. "I got this one," Malia says. She walks onto the court and waits for the players to join her. As the East Side team leaves the bench, Flo high fives a teammate. She glances at Malia, and the two make eye contact. Malia nods. Flo doesn't return the gesture.

This is going to be a weird one, thinks Malia.

With both teams in their positions, Malia takes a deep breath and walks into the centre circle. She checks in with Gina, who nods to signal she's ready. Malia throws the ball in the air. It sails upward directly between the two players. They jump. The East Side player taps the ball to Flo's teammate Tilda, and the game begins.

***

Midway through the second quarter, Malia can feel the energy on the court. Boundary's Number 12 takes a shot. It soars through the air, but clanks off the rim. Flo and Boundary's Number 14 compete to grab the rebound. Number 14 gets her hands on the ball first and brings it toward her body. But Flo doesn't give up. She bats at the ball. A moment later, it pops out of the Boundary player's hand. It skims Flo's leg before it bounces out of bounds.

The action is taking place in Gina's zone. She blows the whistle and makes a gesture. "East Side ball."

"What a surprise," says Boundary's coach sarcastically. "Are any of the calls going to go our way?"

Malia doesn't react, but in her head she knows the coach is right. All of Gina's judgement calls have favoured East Side.

Gina hands the ball to Tilda out of bounds. East Side runs a play. Flo is open under the basket. Tilda passes her the ball. Flo shoots and scores.

Malia feels a little surge of pride course through her

body. She shakes her head, trying to shimmy the feeling way.

Neutral. She's supposed to be neutral.

Two minutes later, the half-time horn sounds. Gina and Malia meet at the scorekeepers' table to drink water.

"Who knew a grade-seven girls' game could be so intense?" Gina looks around the gym. "The East Side–Boundary rivalry probably has something to do with it, eh?"

"Probably," says Malia. She looks at Anna and Maria. "How are you two doing? Everything okay?"

"It's fast," says Anna nervously. "I think I might have given two points to the wrong player." She points at the detailed score sheet.

Malia bends so that she's eye-level with Anna. "Individual points aren't that important. The team stuff and individual fouls are what matter." Anna nods seriously. "You're doing great," Malia adds.

The horn sounds to signal the beginning of the second half. The half-time break hasn't disrupted the game's intensity. The players begin the third quarter as fiercely as they ended the second.

Throughout the third and fourth quarter, the game remains close. In the last minute of the fourth and final quarter, the game is tied.

Tilda receives the ball on offence in Malia's zone. Malia watches the action closely. Her gaze is focussed enough to note details but soft enough to see all the players she needs to. Tilda fakes a shot. Her defender jumps, and Tilda blows past her. Tilda speeds toward the hoop. But one of the Boundary players sees her coming and puts her body between Tilda and the hoop. If Tilda sees the Boundary player, she doesn't care. She jumps, flying toward the hoop. On the way, she crashes into the Boundary player.

Malia blows her whistle. Both teams look at her expectantly.

"Charge!" yells Boundary's coach.

"Block!" yells East Side's coach.

"Charge," says Malia firmly. She makes the call gesture. "Number 8 on East Side."

In the stands, the East Side fans boo. Malia looks up and sees that it's mostly parents. Parents she knows. She looks back at the court. East Side's coach is flapping like a bird trying to fly. Boundary's coach is directing his team. Flo is glaring at Malia like she's trying to burn a hole through Malia's chest with her eyes.

Malia gulps. She moves to her spot on the sidelines, eager to get the game going again.

"Timeout!" calls Boundary's coach.

Malia nods and blows her whistle. "Timeout, Boundary."

Malia walks to join Gina at centre court.

"Gutsy call," Gina says.

"The Boundary player's feet were set," explains Malia.

"That's one way to see it."

"What's that supposed to mean?"

"It was close," says Gina. "That's all."

The timeout ends, and the players return to the court. The Boundary team inbounds the ball to their best player, Number 6. The other players run to the baseline. Number 6 dribbles the ball calmly, waiting for the clock to tick down. With ten seconds left in the game, she makes a move. She beats her defender. None of the East Side players are in position to stop her. The Boundary player shoots and scores.

Flo gets the ball and passes it inbounds to Tilda. But there isn't enough time left. Tilda is forced to throw the ball from the defensive end toward the offensive basket. It lands well in front of the hoop as the horn sounds.

The Boundary players cheer loudly. Malia bites her lip. She did make the right call, didn't she?

The teams shake hands. As Flo returns to her bench, she passes Malia. "Don't wait for me," she snaps. "I'd rather walk home alone."

Malia thanks Anna and Maria for their work and grabs her bag. She makes her way to the stands and out of the gym. The East Side parents turn away from her as she passes them.

9 The FALLOUT

Malia is on a cafeteria bench, eating her turkey sandwich. She is squished between Priya, who is doing her math homework while eating celery and peanut butter, and Zoe, who twirls her hair while listening to Sean ramble.

". . . right, Priya?" asks Sean. Priya is too caught up in her homework to reply. Sean picks up one of his mini carrot sticks and gently tosses it in Priya's direction. As the carrot flies through the air, Malia reaches out and catches it.

Priya looks up. "Nice hands."

"Thanks," says Malia. She throws the carrot stick in her mouth.

Priya glares at Sean. "What was that for?"

"You didn't answer me."

Priya rolls her eyes. "What did you ask?"

"I said our math teacher assigns too much homework."

"There's a lot."

"See," says Sean, gesturing to the table.

"But it's not out of this world. You just have to do it. And I have soccer after basketball tonight, so I need to do it now." Priya returns to her math homework.

Victor's sister Tilda walks up to the table. "You lost us the game yesterday," she says to Malia bluntly.

Malia hesitates. Her instinct is to point out that Tilda lost her team the game by running over another player. But Tilda is two years younger than Malia. And refs aren't supposed to engage with player complaints. "That's not the way I see it," says Malia carefully.

Tilda looks to her brother for support. "You think so, right?" she asks him.

Victor glances at Malia. "I wasn't there, Tilda."

"But I told you about it. And you heard Mom and Dad talking."

Malia clenches her fist beneath the table.

Victor turns his full attention to Malia, and a gentle warmth fills her body. "Why did you make the call?" Victor asks.

"Because I'm a ref and that's my job?" Malia replies. She checks Victor's expression. Unlike with Tilda, there's no frustration in his eyes. But there isn't understanding either.

"What's this about?" asks Sean.

"Malia was reffing the grade seven game against Boundary yesterday," explains Victor casually. "She called a charge on Tilda at the end of the game.

Boundary got the ball, scored and won the game."

"Was it a charge?" asks Zoe.

"It wasn't," proclaims Tilda.

"It was," says Malia firmly. "But it was close," she concedes.

"So if it was close, why not call it for our team?" asks Sean. "Especially against Boundary." Everyone at the table nods to agree with Sean. "Right, Priya?"

"Yeah," says Priya, distracted.

"See!" says Tilda. She turns and storms away from the table.

As Tilda leaves, Sean guides the conversation back to his favourite topic: the deeply unfair, inhumane, just plain wrong amount of math homework their teacher assigns. But Malia can't focus. She can barely look at her friends. Are they right? If it was close, should she have favoured her school?

Beside Malia, Priya scribbles furiously in her notebook. Malia reaches into her bag and grabs her phone. She sends a text message:

Reffing crisis. Pizza later?

"Who's Carlos?" asks Zoe. Her eyes light up at the chance of a scandal.

Malia tilts her screen away from Zoe's snooping eyes.

"You're texting him?" asks Priya suddenly.

"Oh," says Malia. "So that got your attention." She

grabs her backpack and gets up from the table.

"Where are you going?" Priya asks.

"To get ready for class."

"But lunch doesn't end for ten minutes." Priya is confused. "Should I come with you?"

"It's fine," says Malia. "Finish your homework."

★★★

Malia meets Carlos at a pizza place between the two middle schools. The pizza isn't as good as at Joey's Pizzeria. But Joey's is far closer to East Side, and Carlos and Malia have come to an unspoken agreement to always meet between the two neighbourhoods.

"So what's up?" asks Carlos, as he gobbles down his second piece of pizza.

"Did you hear about the grade-seven girls' game last night?"

"Boundary won." Carlos speaks with a little more pride than Malia would like. "That's all I heard."

"There was a call at the end of the game," says Malia. She corrects herself. "I made a call at the end of the game. A call that . . . kind of . . . affected the game."

"How so?"

Malia whips out her phone. "I asked Gloria if anyone recorded the game. One of the parents did. Apparently, one of the Boundary dads uploads all the games so that parents can access them."

"Oh, I know him," says Carlos fondly. "Intense. But loves his daughters."

"Anyway, Gloria sent me the file." She hands her phone to Carlos, the video cued to right before the foul.

He watches the clip. "Hm," he says seriously. He rewinds the clip and watches it again. Then again. "It's a close call."

"It is," sighs Malia. "In the moment, I was sure her feet were set. But watching it . . . I don't know . . ." She runs her hands through her hair. "It's hard to say."

"The camera angle is also really different from yours on the court."

"I know. But that's not a lot of help. Flo wouldn't talk to me after the game. The East Side parents gave me the cold shoulder. And today at school, Tilda called me out on it in front of my friends."

"Who's Tilda?"

"The offensive player," says Malia as Carlos watches the clip again. "She says I lost her team the game."

Carlos looks up from the video. "She clearly sees the defensive player," he says, thinking aloud. "She could have stopped and shot rather than risking a foul."

"And I could have made a different call."

"You could've," says Carlos. "But you didn't make the wrong call. It's like Gloria said. It was a judgement call."

"One that lost my school team the game against . . ." she looks up at Carlos, "our rival school," she finishes and sighs. "I don't know. Maybe I'm not meant to be a ref."

"Is anyone meant to be a ref?"

"Gloria might be."

"She makes mistakes, too."

"Maybe."

Carlos furrows his eyebrows and goes silent for a moment. Then he stares at Malia intensely.

"What are you doing?" asks Malia.

"Thinking. Hold on." Carlos narrows his gaze. Suddenly, he opens his eyes wide. "Got it!"

"Got what?"

"It's just like taking a game-winning shot," Carlos explains. "Even though it might feel like it, a single shot never wins or loses a game. There were hundreds of shots that came before it. Same with fouls. No single call wins or loses a game."

"I guess . . ."

"Would more pizza help? Pizza always helps me. We could split a piece?"

Malia nods, and Carlos hops up from the table to order another slice. Malia watches the clip again, hoping to see something new. But it's the same. At the end of the day, it was Malia's choice to make the call. And now she must live with the consequences.

Where was that in the reffing manual?

10 BAD DAY

Malia yawns as she walks into East Side through the front doors. Still groggy, she meanders through the hallway. Her basketball shoes are tied to the top of her bag so she won't forget them for the game after school. They bounce against her shoulders as she walks. Malia passes two grade seven girls, and they glare at her. Malia stares right back. After eating two more pieces of pizza and talking to Carlos, Malia decided that she's annoyed with her friends for not seeing her side. And that she's not going to let her little sister's friends bother her. Especially not before nine in the morning.

When Malia gets to her locker, Priya is waiting for her. Priya's eyes are bright and awake. "Did you hear?"

"Mm?" says Malia. She slowly turns the combination lock.

"Grade nine boys' game last night. East Side versus Boundary."

"What about it?"

"Victor got hurt."

"What?" Malia turns to Priya. "How?"

"He stole the ball on defence. Had a wide-open layup. The Boundary players couldn't catch up. So one of them shoved him last minute. Just as he jumped. Victor landed on his wrist. He's getting x-rays today. It was totally on purpose, and all the Boundary boys were laughing about it."

"Were you there?"

Priya shakes her head. "Cross-country practice. But I heard the whole thing from Zoe."

"Right."

"And that's not all. There was a fight in the parking lot after the game. Sean and Mirza sent those Boundary boys a message."

Malia nods. "Was anyone hurt?"

"Not seriously. I think it was just a bunch of pushing and shoving. Parents were still around. They stopped it. But I bet the Boundary players think twice before attacking one of our guys again."

"Yeah . . ." Malia pulls her morning books out of her bag.

"Why are you so calm? Victor, *your* Victor, got attacked."

"He's not *my* Victor."

"You like him," challenges Priya.

Malia bites her lip. When she's around Victor, it's like she's a phone being charged. She feels like a power surge runs through her. But he didn't even try to listen to Malia at lunch. What good is a power surge with someone who doesn't have your back?

"Or . . ." Priya's tone softens. "Do you like Carlos now?"

"What?"

"The Boundary boy." Her tone isn't accusing. She sounds curious, concerned. "You've been talking to him a lot. You should be careful there. He could have been the player that attacked Victor."

"He wasn't."

"How do you know?"

"Because he doesn't play. And he was having pizza with me."

"What?! Why didn't you tell me?"

"I needed to talk and you were at soccer."

"But I had to go to soccer practice."

"Of course you did," says Malia. "And you can't be in two places at once."

Priya looks at the ground. "It'd be better if I could be."

The bell rings.

"Come on," says Malia. "I'll walk you to English on my way to History."

***

In her basketball game against West Side, Malia jumps to grab an offensive rebound. The West Side players aren't very talented, but they're tall. Malia soars into the air, but West Side Number 16's arms are longer. She plucks the ball out of mid-air and brings it to her chest.

Malia lands and runs back on defence.

Number 16 passes the ball to her point guard, Number 7. Zoe charges toward Number 7 to defend her. Number 7 starts to dribble the ball up the court, using her non-dribbling hand to protect the basketball. As Zoe defends, she places a hand on Number 7's hip.

"Hand off," warns the ref, whistle between her teeth. Number 7 keeps dribbling, but Zoe's hand doesn't move. The ref blows her whistle. "Foul. East Side Number 14. Hand Check."

Zoe looks to the ceiling and grunts. Coach Lucy yells down the bench, and Valentina runs to the scorekeepers' table to substitute in for Zoe.

The play resumes. West Side Number 7 gets the ball on the wing. She passes to Number 6 and then Number 16. Priya lunges to steal the final pass, but misses. Number 16 charges toward the basket. Valentina runs over to stop her. The two players jump into the air, making contact.

The ref blows her whistle. "Foul. East Side Number 20."

"Come on!" yells Coach Lucy from the bench. "The offence initiated the contact."

Valentina's shoulders slump as the players line up for the free throws.

"Don't worry about it," says Malia supportively. "You'll get the next one."

Number 16 scores her first free throw, but misses her second. Priya swoops in and catches the rebound. She passes the ball to Malia who dribbles it up the court, looking for her teammates. She passes the ball to Lauren. Lauren fakes a shot and drives toward the hoop. She beats her defender, but another West Side defender steps in. Malia makes a hard cut to the basket. Lauren passes her the ball. Malia reaches out and grabs it. She takes one hard dribble and then jumps toward the hoop. A West Side player reaches out to try to block her, but she misses and hits Malia's wrist. The ball bobbles in Malia's hand. But she regains control and manages to direct it toward the rim.

The ball clanks on the front of the rim and rolls through the net. Off-balance, Malia falls to the side. She looks up at the ref expectantly but no call is made.

"Foul!" screams Coach Lucy from the bench.

Still nothing from the ref. Malia hops up and runs back on defence. Before West Side can shoot, the horn signals the end of the second quarter. Malia and her teammates make their way off the court and gather in the corner for half-time.

Coach Lucy strides toward the ref before joining them. Malia can tell from her firm gestures that she isn't asking the ref how her day is going. When she's done pointing at the ref, Coach Lucy joins the team.

"There are lots of good things to take from that first half," begins Coach Lucy. She outlines player and team successes. "If we keep up the energy and execute our plays, we can win this game." She glances at the refs. "And, hopefully, the calls will be a bit more even this time round."

"The refs are brutal," agrees Zoe.

"I've seen better," says Coach Lucy. "But that's for me to worry about. You just need to play."

"It's hard when they call everything against us," says Valentina.

"And nothing *for* us," adds Priya. She looks at Malia. "You should have gotten a foul shot on that last play."

Malia shrugs. She looks over at the refs. They stare at the two teams nervously. Boy, does she know that feeling. "They're doing their best."

"Really?" says Valentina.

"Yeah, come on, Mal," says Zoe. "Be on our side on this one. Their best isn't good enough."

Malia thinks about her own reffing and shrugs. "Sometimes it isn't."

Her teammates look at her, confused.

"Let's cheer," says Priya, trying to break the tension. She walks over and puts her hand on Malia's shoulder so that the two are standing together. "The refs aren't going to win us the game. We are!"

"Yeah!" agrees the team.

Malia puts her hand in the circle and half-heartedly joins her teammates for the cheer.

★★★

Malia walks through the front door after the game. "I'm home!"

"In the kitchen!" calls her mom. Malia takes off her shoes and goes to the kitchen where her mom is unpacking a frozen pizza.

"How was the game?" her mom asks. "Sorry I couldn't make it. Shift went late."

"It's okay. The first half was close. But we ended up winning by fifteen."

"That's great!"

"It's something."

Her mom gives her a look. "Well, let me know if you want to talk about that something. In the meantime, you got mail." She walks to the counter, shuffles through a bunch of paper and hands Malia an envelope.

Malia opens it. Inside there is a crisp cheque written in Malia's name. The amount is more than a quarter of her season's fees. Malia looks at her mom. Her sleeves are rolled up. There are bags under her eyes, and she's still wearing her work shoes.

"Right," mutters Malia. "I'm reffing for the fee."

"What?" asks her mom.

"Never mind."

"Normally, I wouldn't let you get away with that 'never mind' stuff. But I'd like to change before dinner. Can you set the table?"

Malia nods. As she puts the forks and knives beside the big porcelain plates, she repeats a single thing over and over in her head. *Reffing is a job. Reffing is a job. Reffing is a job.*

11 NO CALL

Malia looks around the Boundary Middle School gym. It certainly isn't the first time she's been in the gym, either as a player or a ref. She knows the high ceilings and shiny glass backboards, a stark contrast to East Side's dimly lit gym. But it's the first time she's reffing a Boundary versus East Side game here. And it happens to be the final game before playoffs.

She looks up at the stands. They're filled with parents, and a lot of older siblings from both schools. Malia spots Victor sitting between his parents, his sprained wrist cradled close to his chest. She sighs and walks to greet the Boundary scorekeepers.

"Hi, I'm Malia. I'm —"

"The ref?" says one of the girls. Her voice drips with snark.

"Yeah . . . Have you two done this before?"

"Of course."

Malia nods. "Well, if you —"

"You're from East Side, right?"

"I am."

"How come you're allowed to ref the game?"

Malia grits her teeth.

"All right," says Gina, walking over to join Malia. "Malia, you ready for this?"

Malia nods but says nothing. It doesn't matter if she's ready. The game is going to happen, and she's going to be a part of it.

Malia and Gina introduce themselves to the coaches. Having reffed both teams before, it's more a formality than anything. Gina and Malia both hesitate before taking the ball to start the game.

"You want to do the toss?" Gina asks.

"You can do it," says Malia. She glances at the stands a final time. Carlos has entered the gym. He stands at the back of the bleachers. Malia sees he is careful to place himself between the two sets of fans.

Malia takes her position as the players slowly walk toward the centre circle. Flo glances nervously at the stands. Their parents, who both work until late, aren't there. Malia wishes they were. The look on Flo's face tells Malia that she wishes the same.

Gina grabs the ball and walks to the centre circle. She nods at Malia who returns the gesture. They're ready for the game to begin. Gina throws the ball into the air. As usual, the toss is off-kilter, and it favours the East Side team. East Side's player taps the ball to Flo.

No Call

Both teams have improved over the season. The play is faster than it was during the first games. Within minutes, Malia is sweating as she jogs up and down the court to keep up with the pace of play. Flo manages to both dart around the court and direct her teammates to the right spots, playing defence in front of Malia. Flo's check on the Boundary team signals to a teammate that she wants the ball. Seeing this, Flo lunges to deflect the pass. She tips it forward, down the court. Flo and the Boundary player chase after the ball. Flo gets there first. She picks up the ball and races down the court.

"Go, Flo!" cheers a parent from the stands.

"Careful!" yells a voice Malia recognizes as Victor's. "Protect yourself."

Malia follows the play. Her sister passes the ball to her teammate Poppy. Poppy jumps into the air to shoot a layup shot. A Boundary player runs beside her, grazing Poppy's arm lightly. It doesn't disrupt the shot, and Poppy scores.

Behind Malia, a whistle blows.

The players stop and Malia turns. Gina, standing at the other end of the court, yells, "Foul! Number 18 Boundary."

Malia stares at Gina. The call is out of Gina's zone. It was Malia's to make.

Gina doesn't look at Malia as she tells the players, "Get lined up."

Malia jogs over to Gina. She lowers her voice so the players can't hear her. "That wasn't your call."

"Just because I'm in high school doesn't mean I don't know what's happening at my middle school. I heard about the boys' game," says Gina firmly. "We need to send the Boundary players a message."

Malia opens her mouth to disagree, but Gina turns away from her and toward the players. Malia retreats to her position for free throws.

Poppy goes to the free-throw line to shoot her foul shot. Gina passes her the ball. Poppy bounces it twice. She takes a deep breath and bends her legs to shoot. But before she releases the ball, her right foot crosses the free-throw line. It clearly breaks the rules. Malia looks at Gina. It's in her zone. It's her call.

Silence.

Poppy releases the ball.

"Come on!" yells Boundary's coach angrily from the sideline. Gina shakes her head. "You're brutal!" he yells, slamming his clipboard on the ground.

Gina blows her whistle. "Technical foul."

A technical foul? *Those are only given if a coach or player says or does something inappropriate*, thinks Malia. Usually refs give a warning before calling a technical foul.

"How dare —" begins the coach. But his assistant grabs his arm and leads him away from Gina. In the stands, the Boundary parents roar with displeasure.

"You're terrible, ref!"
"Brutal!"

★★★

The horn finally sounds to signal the end of the game. Malia doesn't even look up at the clock. She beelines it to the scorekeepers' table. The scorekeepers glare at her as she grabs her bag. Malia keeps her head down as she walks into the bleachers.

"Hey," says Victor, forcing Malia to stop.

"Hi."

"Intense game. Our girls really had to earn that win."

'Earn' isn't the word Malia would use to describe how East Side won the game. Victor can't think what happened during the game was okay, can he?

"And you were super great," he goes on. He reaches to squeeze Malia's forearm. Usually, the gesture would send a jolt of energy through Malia's body. But this time, she feels annoyed. "Do you want to —"

Malia notices the Boundary parents walking toward her and Victor. "I have to go," she says quickly. "But I'll see you tomorrow."

"Okay."

Malia jogs up the stairs to the back of the gym. She speed-walks out of the school. When she gets to the parking lot, she's grateful for the fresh air and the silence.

"Malia," says a voice behind her. Malia turns.

"Carlos," she says, relieved that it isn't a Boundary player or parent.

"What was that?" He strides toward her. "Gina threw the game."

Malia closes her eyes. "I know."

"And you're okay with that?"

"What was I supposed to do?"

"I don't know," sputters Carlos. "You could have . . . overturned her calls."

"We're not supposed to do that."

"Well, she's not supposed to favour one team. You could have at least tried to even things out."

"How?"

"I don't know . . . by making some calls for Boundary. Or," he says mockingly, "is your East Side pride too big for that?"

His words are like a cannon ball. They hit Malia right in the chest and knock the wind out of her.

Carlos's expression falls. "I didn't mean that."

"Of course you did," snaps Malia. "Priya was right. You're just like all the other Boundary kids."

"What's that supposed to mean?"

"It means that if you played basketball, you prob-ably would have shoved Victor from behind and then laughed about it."

"Are we talking about the grade-nine boys' game, now?" replies Carlos. "Because, yes, Steve shoved . . . what's his name . . . Victor? And he shouldn't have done that. But no one laughed. The coach subbed Steve out and yelled at him."

"That's not what I heard."

"Well, it's what I heard. And then your friends attacked Steve in the parking lot. Over something that happened in a basketball game."

"And here you are," says Malia, looking Carlos directly in the face, "yelling at me in a parking lot over something that happened in a basketball game."

Carlos freezes, his eyes wide when he sees the truth in what she said.

"I'm going home." Malia turns and doesn't look back. She quickly unlocks her bike and makes her way home. Tears fall down her cheeks as she rides.

When she gets home, Flo is sitting on the couch. "We won!" she says proudly.

"You did."

"Aren't you happy about it?"

"You played well," says Malia.

"I can play better," says Flo, determined. "I'll have to if we're going to beat them in playoffs. Coach said we play them first round. Best-of-three series. Just got to beat 'em two more times."

Malia goes to the family computer and plops down in the hard chair. She checks her email. There's a message from Gloria titled "Playoff Schedule." Malia clicks on it, and the moment she sees the content, tears well in her eyes again.

"You okay?" asks Flo carefully.

"No."

"What's wrong?"

"I'm scheduled to ref your playoff series."

12 PLAYOFF SCHEDULE

"You know what I think?" asks Priya. She and Malia are walking from the French classroom to the cafeteria. "I think Northern is a good first-round playoff match-up for us. They're not tall like West Side, and they're not as skilled as Boundary. They're just tough. We're from East Side. We can out-tough tough."

"Especially this season," counters Malia. "We've had players foul out of almost every game."

Priya glances at Malia out of the side of her eye. But she doesn't retort. "Are you going to Sean's party on Friday?" she says, changing the subject.

"I think so. You?"

Priya nods tentatively.

"Something wrong?" Malia asks.

"It's my night off this week," sighs Priya. "But I said I'd go, so . . ."

"Do you need the rest?"

"Probably," says Priya. "Not sure one night is going to make a difference at this point. And I don't want to let anyone down."

"I hear that." Malia doesn't want to let anyone down either. But no matter what she does, someone is always unhappy. "But maybe you have to, so that you don't let yourself down?"

"Maybe," says Priya with a tired shrug.

The girls enter the cafeteria. Flo, Tilda and several of their friends wait at Malia's usual table.

"You're reffing our playoff series," states Tilda.

Malia looks at Flo. "You told everyone?"

"You didn't say I couldn't," says Flo.

"We need to talk about this," says Tilda. "Can we trust you to —"

"We're not having this conversation," says Malia. Tilda opens her mouth to protest. "I'm serious. It's against the rules. What's more, I don't want to." She signals to the doors. "Get out of here."

"It's our cafeteria, too," counters Tilda.

Malia takes a step forward. She gets close enough to remind the grade sevens that she's older, taller and stronger than they are. But not so close as to pose a real threat. She looks at Flo. "You know how I said grade nines don't bite? I take that back."

"Come on, Tilda," says Flo. "Let's go. There's no talking to her when she's like this."

The grade sevens leave the cafeteria.

"They're going to be such big games," begins Sean, excitedly. "And I'm not suspended anymore so I can go.

I'm going to be so loud in the stands. I can cheer for you," he says to Malia. "But only if you make good calls."

"Can we talk about something else?" says Malia through gritted teeth.

"Don't worry, Malia," says Victor with a wink. "We know whose side you're on."

"I'm not on anyone's side," snaps Malia.

Victor's eyes go wide. He looks at her expectantly, as if he's waiting for an apology. But why should Malia be sorry? She rips her focus away from Victor's puppy dog expression.

"Sean," says Malia, shifting the group's attention. "How was Math today? Is there a lot of homework?"

"Oh my God," says Sean. "So much and . . ."

Priya tries to make eye contact with Malia but Malia avoids it.

Do her friends really think it's okay for officials to play favourites? She looks around the table and instantly knows the answer. They do when it helps them. But what about if it helped the Boundary team? They'd be furious. And rightfully so. It would be unfair. *Why doesn't that matter when it's the other way around?* thinks Malia. *Why do the two schools dislike each other so much anyway?*

★★★

Malia hustles to keep up with Priya, who is charging down the hallway after school. "I've got to get to soccer.

But we should hang out later," says Priya over her shoulder.

"Don't you have cross country later?"

"After that. Maybe." She pushes through the door, sees her mom's car and jogs toward it. "I'll text you."

Priya hops in the front seat. As they drive away, Malia notices Carlos standing at the edge of the school parking lot. *He looks nervous*, Malia thinks. He hesitates for a moment. But then walks right up to her.

"Hi," he says carefully. "I'm glad I caught you."

"What are you doing here?"

"I would have texted. But I wasn't sure you'd answer." He looks at the ground, then back up at Malia. "I'm sorry about yesterday. I shouldn't have talked to you after the game like that."

"Thanks." Malia looks at Carlos. It surprises her that his presence makes her feel better. "I'm sorry, too. I shouldn't have said some of the things I said, either."

Carlos nods. "I was thinking . . ." he said. "You always say there's a good pizza place around here. My treat?"

"Sure."

Malia leads Carlos away from the school toward Joey's Pizzeria.

"I saw the playoff schedule," says Carlos quietly.

"Yeah . . ."

"How do you feel about it?"

"Not great," says Malia honestly. She looks over her

shoulder at the school. No one would recognize Carlos if they saw him. What would her friends think if they knew? Nothing good, that's for sure. But why? Carlos hasn't done anything to them. "Why are things the way they are between our schools?" she asks.

"Dunno," says Carlos. "I never thought about it until I met you."

Malia leads him into Joey's. The smell of freshly cooked ham and pineapple pizza fills their nostrils. They grab two slices and find a table near the back.

Carlos takes his first bite. "Oh, man. This is good." He greedily takes another bite.

"You've really never been here before?"

"Nope. Never really been in this neighbourhood before."

Malia stiffens. "Right."

"Have you been in mine?"

"I guess not," she says. The stiffness leaves her body as she exhales. "But we live in different parts of the city."

"We don't, really," says Carlos. "You can walk between our schools. I just did it," he points out.

"Did it feel weird being at East Side during school hours?"

"Honestly?" he says, taking a bite of his crust. "A bit. After what happened with Steve and everything. I'm tall," he says with a chuckle. "But I'm not exactly tough."

"Maybe you are," says Malia, smiling. "And you just don't know it."

"Not tough the way East Side boys are."

"How are East Side boys tough?" asks Malia. This time, it's Carlos who freezes. "Not an attack," says Malia. "Just a question."

Carlos knits his eyebrows together as he thinks about it. "I don't know . . . I guess, I've just always been told they are."

"The same way I've been told Boundary boys can't be trusted."

"And then a Boundary kid shoves an East Side kid from behind. Which probably didn't help that."

"And Sean started a fight in a parking lot. And it just makes it worse."

"Do you think there's any chance of making it better?"

"I think you coming here," she says, gesturing at the restaurant, "is making it not worse."

"Not worse isn't exactly better."

"But it's a start." Malia takes a bite of her own pizza. "Hey, I've got an idea. Sean's throwing a party on Friday. Want to come?"

"Sean? The guy who pushed Steve?"

"I hear you," says Malia. "But Sean is actually a doofus. And he wouldn't hurt you." She hesitates. "If you come with me."

Carlos bites his lip.

"I get if you don't want to," says Malia quickly. "I just thought it might be a good way to relax before playoffs. I've got my games and my sister's games. You've got playoff games, too. And who is going to make this better if not us?"

13 AGGRESSIVE DEFENCE

Sweat drips down Malia's cheek as she sprints down the court in a scrimmage at the end of Friday's practice. Lauren, her scrimmage teammate, passes the ball to Penelope. But before Penelope can catch it, Zoe darts out and taps the ball down the court. She runs after it and picks it up. Like in the chase layup drill, Malia sprints after her. Zoe jumps to shoot a layup shot. Malia takes another step and extends her arm. She jumps into the air and reaches for the ball. Her arm grazes Zoe's. But she manages to get a hand on the ball, tipping it out of bounds.

"Foul!" proclaims Zoe.

"I call the fouls," says Coach Lucy. Zoe waits expectantly. "White team ball. Out of bounds."

Zoe groans.

Was it a foul? It was certainly close. But what's a player supposed to do in that situation? Malia remembers her reffing training. All players have a right to the space above and below their feet. But Zoe was jumping forward . . .

Coach Lucy hands the ball to Zoe's teammate Sacha out of bounds.

The problem with the chase play is that the defensive player is behind the offensive player. So the defensive player is always reaching into the offensive player's space.

Sacha passes the ball inbounds.

Malia is hit with the answer. The defensive player needs to get in front of the offensive player! They need to use their feet to get to the right spot rather than reaching with their hands.

Lauren, Malia's check, sprints toward the basket. Her movement pulls Malia out of her thoughts. Malia takes a step, but it's too late. Lauren receives the ball and scores an easy shot.

"Focus, Malia," says Coach Lucy. She blows her whistle. "All right, team, that's it for today's practice. You've got a big weekend coming up. Your last chance to rest before playoffs. Use it wisely and I'll see you all on Monday!"

The team cheers.

Priya jogs out of the huddle to her bag.

Malia plops down on the bench and unties her basketball shoes. Zoe sits down beside her. "You going to Sean's tonight?" asks Zoe.

"That's the plan," replies Malia.

"Want to get ready with Penelope and me?"

"I'd love to, but I can't. I'm bringing someone."

"Who?"

"My friend Carlos."

"Oooooo. He your boyfriend?"

"It's not like that."

"He goes to Boundary," says Priya.

"What?!" yelps Zoe.

Priya looks over her shoulder. Her mom stands at the top of the bleachers. "Ugh!"

"What's up?" asks Malia.

"Can't find my water bottle." Priya's eyes dart around the gym. "Going to be late for my soccer game. My teammates are going to be so mad."

"I'm sure it'll be okay," says Malia.

"I don't know," says Zoe. "I wouldn't be too happy if you were coming late to our games because of a soccer practice."

"I know," says Priya, looking around frantically.

"Real helpful, Zoe," mutters Malia. She reaches out and gently takes Priya's wrist, turning her friend toward her. "You're a great soccer player, so of course your teammates want you at the game. But you're also a great basketball player. You've got a duty to more than one team. Your soccer teammates need to understand that. And if they don't, that's their problem. Not yours."

Priya nods tentatively.

"I'll look for your water bottle," Malia says. "You go to soccer."

Malia begins searching for Priya's water bottle.

"Are you seriously bringing someone from Boundary to Sean's tonight?" asks Zoe.

"I am."

"Does Sean know?"

"Yes. Carlos is not on any of the teams. Sean said it was fine." Zoe raises an eyebrow. "As long he sticks with me," Malia mutters, "which he will. He doesn't know anyone else."

"I can't believe you're doing that," says Zoe like Malia has done something to hurt her.

"Doing what? Inviting one of my friends to hang out with my other friends?"

"I bet he's a spy. Why else would a Boundary boy want to talk to you?"

"Oh, I don't know," says Malia. She stands up and looks around the gym for Priya's water bottle. "Because I'm awesome?"

Zoe tilts her head to the side. "Well I guess that explains why you've been favouring Boundary when you ref."

"What?"

"We all know about the call against Victor's sister."

"It was one call."

"A call that changed the game. That boy has gotten to you."

Malia spots Priya's water bottle under the basketball rack. "Whatever," she says. "I'll see you tonight."

"You're being used, Malia. And you just don't see it."

"And the only thing you see," says Malia pointedly,

"is the school name on the front of his sweatshirt."

Zoe shrugs. Malia shakes her head as she goes to get Priya's water bottle.

★★★

Malia stands outside Sean's front step. She turns to Carlos. "Ready?"

"No one's going to beat me up, right?"

"No," she nudges Carlos. "Or I'll beat them up."

"I'm safe then," he says with a smile.

Malia knocks.

"Come in!" she hears from inside.

Malia and Carlos open the door and head in. The living room is filled with people. "Hey, Mal!" says Sean brightly. He looks at Carlos. "And you."

"Thanks for inviting me."

"I didn't invite you. Malia did."

"Thanks for saying yes, Sean," says Malia.

"He's your friend," Sean shrugs. "It was the right thing to do."

Malia sees Victor and Zoe sitting on the couch. "Come on," she says to Carlos. "I'll introduce you to people."

As Malia and Carlos walk toward the couch, Zoe hops up. "I want some water."

"Me, too," adds Victor. He gets up and follows Zoe to the kitchen.

"Well, we're here now," Malia says to Carlos. "We might as well sit."

Malia sits down. Carlos follows. Within minutes, their corner of the living room is completely empty.

"This is stupid," says Malia. She looks at the kitchen brimming with bodies.

"I can leave," offers Carlos. "So that you can hang out with your friends."

"No!" says Malia, far louder than she intends.

"Or not," he says quickly.

"You can go if you want to," says Malia, disheartened. "I see why you'd want to."

There's a knock at the door.

"Come in!" yells Sean.

Moments later, Priya walks into the living room.

"Hey!" says Malia from the couch. "That's Priya," she explains to Carlos.

"Cool. Think she'll talk to us?"

"Of course."

Like a police officer looking at a crime scene, Priya surveys the living room. She waves at Malia and walks toward the kitchen.

A fire lights in Malia's chest. How dare Priya ignore her!

"Nope," says Malia, shaking her head. "She absolutely cannot do that." She puts her hand on the couch cushions and pushes herself to her feet. "Stay here. I'll be back."

"Where are you going?"

"To talk to Priya," says Malia angrily.

"Talk or yell?"

"Both."

"Is that a good idea?"

Malia looks at the kitchen. Her friends notice that she's standing. They look at her, eyes filled with judgement. "I don't care."

14 The PARTY

Malia squeezes her way through the kitchen. She inches up to Priya, who is at the sink pouring herself a glass of water.

"We need to talk," announces Malia.

Priya turns to face Malia. She blinks several times, as if Malia's voice has pulled her out of a deep sleep. "Huh?"

Sean turns the volume on the radio up. Around Malia, people start to move to the beat.

"We need to talk," repeats Malia loudly.

"Okay."

Brent, who is bopping his head to the beat, accidentally bumps into Malia.

"Somewhere else," Malia adds. The girls manoeuvre their way out of the kitchen and into a hallway that leads to the washroom and the bedrooms. All the bedroom doors are shut. "Washroom it is then." She pulls Priya into the washroom and shuts the door behind them.

Priya looks at Malia curiously. Then her expression changes. "You're angry."

"Of course I'm angry! I bring Carlos to the party and no one will talk to him. Or me. And it's not like I didn't expect that," says Malia. She is half thinking-out-loud, half venting. "I mean I hoped people might at least try. Especially you. But then you walk in and join everyone else."

"I was just —" begins Priya, shakily.

But Malia doesn't let her explain. "Do you have any idea how hard this week has been for me? With the games last week and then the playoff series next week? And we have our own games, too. And everyone's like 'Malia, you have to be on our side,'" she says mocking Victor's tone from earlier in the week. "But who's on my side? It's supposed to be you."

Suddenly, Priya's bottom lip begins to quiver. The quiver quickly turns into a full-out shake. Within seconds, Priya is bawling.

This is not what Malia was expecting.

"I'm sorry," cries Priya. "I saw you and Carlos on the couch and everyone else in the kitchen. It seemed easier to go where everyone else was. And I was just so thirsty and so tired." She sniffles loudly. "I haven't been a very good friend lately. I'm sorry."

Malia looks at her best friend. There are giant bags under her watery eyes. Malia's heart breaks a little. "Thanks."

"I'm just so tired," says Priya sadly. Malia offers her a tissue, and Priya wipes the tears from her cheeks. She takes a deep breath to steady herself. "I feel like I'm being pulled in two hundred directions: soccer, cross-country, school, friends, basketball . . ." Priya stops suddenly. "But this isn't about me. This is about you."

"We can talk about you, too."

Priya nods. "We will. But now it should be about you. I'm sorry that everyone's being awful. I mean, I get why they're being bad with him. But they shouldn't do that to you."

"They shouldn't do it to him, either," counters Malia. "Because they don't know him." Priya opens her mouth to disagree. "And neither do you."

"I know he's from Boundary."

"You also know he's my friend. And," says Malia with a wink, "I have really good taste in friends."

"You do," says Priya, smiling. "You're right. I'll talk to him."

"Thank you."

"I'm not promising anything, though."

"You don't have to. Just try."

Priya looks at herself in the mirror. Her face is puffy from crying. She turns on the tap and splashes water on her face. She dries off with a nearby towel and looks at her reflection again. "That's as good as it's going to get, I guess. Let's go."

The girls leave the washroom and walk down the

hallway. As they're about to turn into the kitchen, they run into Victor.

"Malia!" says Victor. "I was just looking for you."

Malia glances toward the living room, but she can't see through the sea of people.

"Stay," says Priya with a knowing eyebrow wiggle. "I'll check on Carlos." She marches into the crowd and disappears.

"It's hot in here," says Victor. "Want to get some air?"

"Sure," says Malia.

Victor grabs Malia's hand and leads her out the front door. If she could control her heartbeat, she would try to slow it down. They sit on Sean's stoop.

"So," asks Victor smoothly, "excited for next week's games?"

"The ones I'm playing or the ones I'm refereeing?"

"Both."

"Super excited for our games," says Malia honestly. "Northern is a good draw for us. I think we can beat them in two games."

"Of course you will," says Victor, smiling brightly. "You girls are awesome."

"Thanks."

"And the grade-seven games?"

"Nervous."

"There's nothing to be nervous about," says Victor. "Everyone says you're a good ref."

"No one's saying that to me."

"Well, they should be," he says. A softness fills Victor's eyes. He leans toward Malia. Malia's heart pounds in her chest. "And they will." He leans closer, as though he might kiss her. "When you help the grade seven girls next week."

Malia pulls away. "What?"

"You know," he says. The smoothness of his voice suddenly makes Malia's stomach sink. "When you give our sisters a little extra help."

Does Victor truly believe she'd do that? Another even worse thought races through Malia's mind. Is that what he's trying to persuade her to do?

Tears well in her eyes. She hops up.

"Where are you going?" asks Victor, confused. Malia doesn't look back. "Is everything okay?"

Malia walks into the house and heads into the living room. Priya and Carlos are sitting on the couch, chatting. When they notice Malia, they both go to her.

"What happened?" asks Priya.

"Victor . . ." Malia can't get the words out without crying.

"Did he hurt you? Because if he did, I'm going to break his other wrist," says Priya angrily.

"It's fine." Malia quickly puts on her shoes. "I just want to go home."

"Well, I'm leaving, too, then."

"Me, too," adds Carlos.

Malia doesn't wait for Priya and Carlos to put on their shoes before storming out of the door. She passes Victor on the stoop, and makes her way onto the street.

"Malia," says Priya gently when she and Carlos catch up. "What happened?"

Feelings of hurt, betrayal and embarrassment fuel Malia as she marches down the street. Priya and Carlos hustle to keep up.

"He . . ." Malia's eyes fill with tears. She swallows thickly. "Victor asked me to sit on the porch with him. And he was being really nice. I thought he was going to . . ." She can't say the word 'kiss.' "But then he brought up Flo's game. He said he wanted me to cheat for East Side."

"That jerk!" exclaims Priya.

"I think it's the reason he wanted to sit with me," says Malia through her tears. "He was trying to influence me."

"We don't know that," says Carlos carefully. "Maybe he just —"

"Just what?" asks Malia as she reaches the edge of her driveway.

"Maybe he's just . . . stupid?" offers Carlos.

"Oh, he's stupid," says Priya. "If he thinks I'm going to let him get away with that. I should go back to that party right now and —"

"Don't," pleads Malia. She looks at her house. "I just

want to go to bed and wake up and not have even more drama to deal with."

"I don't want to leave you," says Priya.

"Me either," adds Carlos.

Malia sighs. "How about we go to the high-school game tomorrow morning? All three of us? We can talk more then." Priya and Carlos look at each other and nod. "I'll see you in the morning."

"Text if you need anything," says Priya as Malia walks toward her door.

"What she said," echoes Carlos.

15 WORTH IT?

Malia wakes up on Saturday morning and rubs her eyes. They're puffy and dry from crying herself to sleep. She rolls over slowly and checks her phone. There are messages from both Priya and Carlos.

She pushes herself out of bed. Her feet drag along the carpet as she makes her way to her door. She turns into the hallway to go to the washroom.

"I can't believe you," says Flo from the door of her own bedroom. "Bringing that Boundary boy to your party last night."

"Not now, Flo," says Malia shakily.

"Now." Flo strides up to Malia so she's standing directly in front of her. "Do you have any idea how much the games this week mean to me?"

"The games are important?" Malia can't keep the sarcasm out of her voice. "Gee, I had no idea."

"You think you're funny?"

"How do you even know about the party last night?"

"Tilda told me." An image of Victor flashes through Malia's mind. Tears well in her eyes. "So, what?" Flo continues. "You're going to throw the game for Boundary now? Because of some boy? I'm your sister!"

"I'm not going to throw the game for anyone."

"That's not what Victor thinks," Flo snarls. "I think you're jealous because I'm going to be better than you, and you're trying to stop me! You care more about yourself than anything else. You're selfish and —"

"Shut up!" screams Malia.

"Malia!" says her mom, suddenly appearing at the top of the stairs.

"Flo started it."

"That's not an excuse to speak to your sister that way."

"It's not an excuse, but it's a good reason," snaps Malia. She looks at Flo. "I'm only doing this for you, you know!"

"Doing what?" sneers Flo. "Cheating?"

"Reffing. I signed up for the course so I could pay my own fees. So that *you* could play basketball. And what do I get for it? Nothing. All anyone ever does is yell at me and judge me and try to use me!"

"Oh, Mal . . ." says her mom.

Malia stomps to the washroom and slams the door shut.

Despite her mother's best efforts to stop her, half an hour later Malia slips out of the house and goes to the high school. She walks into the gym, and sees Carlos and Priya standing together. In the crowd of high-school parents and players, no one seems to care that Priya's wearing an East Side sweater and Carlos is wearing a Boundary one.

"How are you doing?" asks Priya.

"Not great," says Malia honestly. The three make their way into the gym. "I got in a fight with Flo this morning."

They sit at the top of the bleachers. Malia notices that Gloria is one of the refs. The horn sounds to signal a minute left until the beginning of the game.

"Tilda told her I brought you to the party last night," explains Malia to Carlos.

"I'm just one big problem, eh?" says Carlos.

"You could say that," says Priya.

"Priya," chides Malia.

"I was kidding." Malia raises an eyebrow. "Half kidding," Priya admits. "I'm still working on this friends-with-Boundary-people thing."

"I'll take working," says Carlos. "Honestly, it sounds to me like this Victor guy is the problem."

"I'm going to kill him," says Priya.

"Please don't," says Malia. "I just want him to go away. I want all of it to go away. But it won't until this playoff series is over."

On the court, Gloria blows her whistle. The players from Vancouver High and Kelowna High, the visiting team, gather on the court. Gloria throws the ball into the air for the jump ball. The Vancouver centre wins the jump ball and taps it to her teammate, Number 18. Vancouver Number 25 sprints down the right side of the court. Number 18 passes the ball to Number 25 who catches it and scores.

"Did they just run a play off the jump ball!?" asks Priya.

"I think so," says Malia.

"Cool."

"The game is so fast," notes Carlos. "Can you imagine reffing these games?"

Malia shakes her head. "I can't even imagine reffing the grade-seven games right now."

"Can't you talk to Gloria?" asks Carlos. "Maybe she could switch the schedule."

"She said she'd only switch the schedule for emergencies. I don't want to risk it. I've almost paid off the fee."

"The fee?"

"Oh," says Malia. She glances at Priya. She can see her friend is holding her breath, waiting to see what Malia will do. "I started reffing so I could pay my basketball fees. I don't want to lose my spot in the rotation."

"That makes sense. Maybe you won't, though?"

"Maybe."

On the court, Vancouver Number 24 and Kelowna Number 16 chase after a rebound. The ball bounces near the sideline. Both players reach for the ball, but neither can grab it. It grazes Vancouver Number 24's leg before going out of bounds.

Gloria's reffing partner blows her whistle. "Out of Bounds. Vancouver ball!"

"What?!" screams the Kelowna coach.

In the stands, the parents boo.

Suddenly, Gloria blows her whistle. She jogs over to her reffing partner and pulls her to the side. The women talk to each other in whispers. A moment later, Gloria blows her whistle and reverses the call. "Kelowna ball!"

Gloria takes the ball and waits patiently for the players to get in position. The game resumes, calmly. For the rest of the game, Malia does something she would have never thought she'd do. She watches the refs rather than the players.

★★★

After the game, Malia, Priya and Carlos walk through the crowded lobby and out the big double doors.

"I was thinking about your scheduling situation, Priya," says Carlos, holding the door open for both girls.

"You were?" asks Priya.

"We talked about it last night."

"I know. I just . . ." She stares at him, confused. Malia thinks Priya looks like she's run into a math problem she doesn't know how to solve.

"I've been meaning to ask about that, too," says

Malia. "How are *you* doing, Priya?"

"I'm tired," says Priya.

"I think you need to talk to your coaches," says Carlos. "There's no way they want one of their best athletes to be exhausted. They should work together to help you pick which practices are the most important and to make sure you have time off."

"How do you know I'm one of their best athletes?" asks Priya.

"Malia told me. Also you play, what, six hundred sports? It would be weird if you were bad at them." They reach the end of the block. "Think about it."

"I will, actually," promises Priya.

"Cool. Well, this is where I turn off. I'll see you both later?"

"For sure," says Malia.

Malia and Priya walk down the street toward their neighbourhood.

"He's weirdly okay," says Priya.

"I know."

"That said, I think he'd take what I'm about to say the wrong way."

"Okay?"

"I was thinking about your games. You're reffing with Gina again, right?" Malia nods. "So chances are she'll do what she's done before and be biased for East Side."

"You don't think that's a problem?"

"I do," says Priya genuinely. "It's wrong, and I get it. But I also think it might take care of a problem for you."

"What do you mean?"

"Before Sean's party, you told me that I had to be responsible for myself."

"That's not exactly what I said."

"It's close enough," says Priya. "And you were right. Sometimes, I have to do what's right for me. Even if it makes other people mad. The tricky part is figuring out what being responsible to myself means. And I think Carlos is right. I don't have to do that alone. Maybe my coaches can help me."

"And what does that have to do with me?"

"Are you responsible for making sure the entire game is fair? Or for doing your best? What if you just ref the game, call what you see and let Gina do her thing? That way, everyone wins."

"I . . ." Malia wants to say she can't do that. But she's already done it once. And Priya isn't wrong. It isn't her job to police Gina. It's Malia's job to call the fouls in her zone and be fair. "Maybe?"

"You're in a really hard position," says Priya. "It's just a thought. I don't know if it's a good one."

"Well, it's better than no thought at all."

"Thanks." Priya sighs. "I'm done thinking about sports for today. Let's watch a movie."

16 The PLAYOFFS BEGIN

Malia taps her fingers against her desk. Her English teacher is explaining something about commas, but Malia can't focus. The grade-nine girls have their first playoff game after school. Last week, Malia felt that Northern was a good first-round match-up. Today she isn't so sure. What if Northern got better since the last time the two teams played? What if they have new plays? Or a new defence? In a three-game series, the first game is really important. What if East Side loses?

The school announcement system crackles. "East Side students, this is your principal. Rather than a bell, I wanted to conclude today with an announcement . . ."

"Does this mean class is over?" asks Riley from the front of the classroom.

The teacher brings her finger to her mouth. "Shhh."

"Several of our basketball teams have qualified for playoffs, and I want to send hearty congratulations to all of them. Excitingly, two of our girls' teams finished high enough during regular-season play to host the first round of playoffs. Today, our grade-nine girls play the Northern Eagles and tomorrow our grade-seven girls play the Boundary Lions. I encourage you all to support your school by attending the games and encouraging our players." She clears her throat. "A reminder that encouragement involves cheering *for* East Side rather than *against* the other team, the officials or anyone else in the gym . . ."

"Says you!" says Riley.

The rest of the class laughs, but Malia winces. Will her friends and schoolmates cheer *against* her in the grade-seven game? Malia knows the answer. If they don't like what they see, yes.

"Go Ducks!" cheers the principal, before turning off the announcement system.

When Malia gets to her locker, Priya is waiting. "What took you so long?"

"Everyone wanted to wish me luck for the game."

"Nice."

The girls make their way to the gym. Even though the game doesn't start for an hour, people are already milling around.

"Hi, girls," says Zoe's dad. The girls nod. "Ready for the big game?"

"Totally," says Priya confidently.

"I hear you're reffing the grade sevens tomorrow," he says, looking at Malia. She nods again. "I think that's great! You getting involved like that."

"Thanks."

"And I want you to know that the East Side parents have your back. We know that the charging call at the beginning of the season was a mistake. You were still learning. You proved that in the final league game. And it's good to know our girls have a little extra support on the court." He pats Malia on the back supportively.

"I —"

"We need to get changed," says Priya quickly. She grabs Malia's wrist and tugs her toward the change room.

"I can't believe he did that," says Malia to Priya in the change room hallway.

"I can. It's Zoe's dad," says Priya. "Don't let it get to you."

"Easy for you to say. He accused me of rigging the final league game."

"He didn't accuse you of anything," says Priya matter-of-factly. "He was proud of you for doing it."

"But I didn't do anything." Malia remembers the technical foul. "Which was the problem." Then Malia remembers Priya's suggestion from Saturday. "I don't know if I can do that again."

"Fair," says Priya. "But maybe you can think about it *after* our game?"

"Yeah," says Malia. She shakes her head. "You're right. Let's do this."

Fifty-five minutes later, Malia stands at the centre

circle. She waits for the ref to toss the ball in the air and begin the game.

"Let's go, East Side!" cheers a parent from the bleachers. The East Side fans, crammed into the nearly full gym, clap loudly.

The ref nods at her partner and walks to the centre circle. She throws the ball into the air. Valentina and Northern Number 33 jump. Valentina gets her hand on the ball first and taps it to Priya. The moment Priya catches the ball, Malia sprints toward the hoop. Priya takes a step, bends her arm and throws a long pass to Malia. Malia catches the ball and shoots.

She keeps her eyes on the rim and watches as the ball tumbles through the mesh. Just as Malia's about to land, a Northern player runs into her side. Malia is lightly pushed off course.

The ref blows her whistle. "Foul! Northern Number 52."

"Nice!" says Priya. The girls high five.

The players line up for Malia's free throw. She dribbles the ball twice, spins it in her hand and then shoots.

She scores!

Good start to the game, thinks Malia. She looks up at the scoreboard, proud of her three points.

Malia runs to her check while Lindsay defends Northern's point guard, Number 45. Dribbling the ball up the court, Number 45 hesitates and rocks her weight onto her heels. Then suddenly, she explodes forward.

Lindsay is caught off guard. Rather than move her feet, she reaches out and attempts to bat the ball away.

The ref blows her whistle. "Reaching foul. Number 12 East Side."

Lindsay sighs.

The scorekeepers record the foul, and play resumes.

A Northern player catches the ball outside the three-point line. She raises the ball as if she's going to shoot. Zoe jumps to block the shot. But the Northern player doesn't shoot. She dribbles past Zoe and goes for the hoop. Priya rushes toward her. The Northern player and Priya jump at the same time. Priya lightly grazes her torso.

The ref blows her whistle. "Foul! East Side Number 6."

After the Northern player's free throws, the game continues. Malia thinks it could be the slowest quarter of basketball she has ever played in. It seems as if the refs call a foul every time they go down the court. When the quarter buzzer finally sounds, Malia is relieved to get a drink of water and a break from the slow pace of play.

"The refs are crazy," says Lindsay in the team huddle. "They're calling everything."

Coach Lucy walks into the huddle.

"We need to stay aggressive," says Zoe. "Not back down."

Coach Lucy looks at a copy of the scoresheet and

sighs. "We're in foul trouble, and it's only been one quarter. Zoe's right, we need to be assertive. But we've got to tone it down a little bit."

The team nods, and the horn sounds for another quarter.

17 CLEAN DEFENCE

"Northern ball," says the ref. She stands at half, the ball in her hand, ready to start the second quarter.

The players line up. A Northern player takes the ball from the ref and passes it inbounds to her teammate Number 45. Lindsay defends Number 45, waving her hands aggressively to try to disrupt the dribbler.

"Remember what we talked about," calls Coach Lucy.

Lindsay takes a step back from the offensive player and stills her hands. With more room, the Northern player has plenty of time to look around and make an easy pass to her teammate. After passing the ball, Number 45 runs toward the hoop. Her teammate passes her the ball and she fires an open shot near the hoop. She scores.

Lauren dribbles the ball up the court. "Line!" she yells, signalling that East Side should set up for the line play. Malia runs to her spot. "Go!"

Malia takes a step toward Lauren, signalling that she's ready to defend the pass. Lauren releases the ball. Malia's defender lunges forward and knocks the ball away. It bounces down the court. The Northern player chases after it. Malia tries to redirect her momentum, but she's too slow. The Northern player picks up the ball. Lauren chases after her. The players run toward the basket. Lauren is fast enough that she's able to catch the Northern player.

Get in front of her, thinks Malia. *Force her to stop.*

Lauren does not try to get in front of the offensive player. Instead, she runs next to the player with the ball. She keeps her distance and puts her hands straight in the air so she can't be called for a foul. The Northern player shoots an easy layup and scores.

"Timeout!" yells Coach Lucy from the sidelines.

The ref blows her whistle. "Timeout, East Side."

The players jog to the bench.

"I know I said that we need to tone things down," says Coach Lucy in the team huddle. "But we can't just *let* them score. We still must work hard and challenge shots."

"What was I supposed to do?" demands Lauren. "If I breathe on the other team, the refs call a foul."

Coach Lucy hesitates. "I wish I had a clear answer for you, but —"

"There is an answer," says Malia. "Play defence properly."

"What's that supposed to mean?" snaps Lauren.

"The refs are calling the game super tight —"

"No kidding," mutters Zoe.

Malia forges on. "But they're not being unfair. Every player has a right to their own space. Even the defenders. But we have to be in the right position first. And we can't reach or slap when we're out of position."

Her team nods, but no one looks convinced.

The horn sounds to signal the end of the timeout.

Play resumes and Lauren dribbles the ball up the court. "Line!" she calls again. Lauren looks at Malia. Her defender shifts her weight, trying to anticipate the pass. Suddenly, Lauren changes direction. She bounces the ball from her right hand to her left hand, and speeds past her defender. Priya's defender steps in to stop her. Lauren makes an easy pass to a wide-open Priya who shoots and scores.

"Good job, girls!" cheers Coach Lucy.

Malia runs back on defence. Number 45 looks in Malia's direction. Malia stays closer to her player, and the point guard turns in the other direction to look for an open teammate. Number 45 passes to Priya's check. Number 45 rocks her weight backward.

She's going to cut toward the basket, thinks Malia.

Malia runs toward the centre of the court. At the same moment, Number 45 cuts. Her teammate releases the ball. Malia jumps into Number 45's path, two steps in front of her. She sets her feet and gets ready for contact. Number 45 bobbles the ball as she catches it. When she finally corrals it, she runs into Malia's chest. Malia falls to the ground.

The ref blows her whistle. "Charge! Northern Number 45."

Priya runs over to help Malia up.

"That's what we have to do," says Malia. "Be in the right spot."

Priya nods. Malia sees that her friend gets what she is showing the team.

Play resumes. Lauren dribbles the ball up the court and East Side runs a play. Zoe gets up for a shot but misses. A Northern player gets the rebound and quickly passes it to Number 45. She sprints down the court, dribbling the ball in front of her. Lauren races to catch up with her, but she's behind the play. Seeing this, Priya sprints down the court. She catches Number 45, but she doesn't step in to defend right away. Instead, she takes three more steps so that her body is directly in Number 45's path. The offensive player stops and looks to pass to a teammate.

"Good D!" encourages Malia.

As the game goes on, Priya and Malia challenge the Northern players by sprinting to the correct spots. Slowly, their teammates follow their lead. By the end of the game, East Side wins by fifteen points.

After shaking hands with the other team and meeting for Coach Lucy's post-game talk, Priya and Malia get ready to leave the gym and go for a victory dinner. Priya looks up at the score clock. She smiles. "I really like winning."

"No kidding," says Malia teasingly.

"And the way we played today . . . if we can do that every game, we really might beat Boundary in the finals."

Students and parents wait in the stands, eager to congratulate the team.

"Need water before going up there," explains Malia, shaking her empty bottle. Malia jogs down the hallway leading to the change room. She hears voices, one of which sounds very familiar.

"What's going on?"

No doubt, thinks Malia. *That's Flo's voice.*

There's a loud sniffle. "Watching the grade-nine game today and seeing everyone in the stands . . . I don't want to play tomorrow."

Malia stops to listen.

"You have to play, Poppy. We need you."

"What if it's like last game?"

"What happened last game?"

"I stepped over the line. And that stupid ref, not your sister, the other one, she made that call. And then that Boundary coach started to yell, and it was all my fault."

"But that's the other team's coach —"

"I play basketball to get away from yelling," Poppy sniffles.

Whoa, thinks Malia.

"I can't. I can't. I can't," says Poppy frantically.

Suddenly, Malia hears a scuffle of sounds and then footsteps. Moments later, Poppy runs past Malia down the hallway.

A moment later, Flo follows. "Poppy —"

"Let her go," says Malia gently. "This is bigger than you."

"Did you hear us?"

"Just the last bit."

"I have to tell my coach what she said, don't I? About the yelling?"

"I can if you want," offers Malia.

"No," says Flo with a sigh. "I think you're doing enough for me." She looks up at Malia with soft eyes. "I didn't know about the fee thing and reffing." She looks at the ground. "I shouldn't have yelled at you the other day. I'm sorry."

"Thanks."

"I just wish you weren't reffing. Then you could just watch me play rather than be part of it."

"I get that."

"You would watch me, right? You wouldn't be one of those horrible sisters that doesn't come to things?"

"Of course I would watch you."

"That's what I thought. I wish things were like that." Flo takes a deep breath like she's about to shoot a free throw. She breathes out slowly. "But they aren't," she concludes. "And I should be better about that. I will be tomorrow."

"Just focus on playing your best," Malia tells her. Flo nods. "Come on. Mom will be waiting, and we've got a lot to update her about."

18 CHAOS

Malia stands at the scorekeepers' table and adjusts her uniform. On the court, the teams warm up. Malia watches as Flo goes through the motions of a simple layup drill: she waits in line, catches the ball, scores a layup and jogs to the next line. She never smiles. Malia turns her attention to the Boundary team. They are also running basic drills with serious expressions plastered on their faces.

In the stands, the fans sit on either side of an invisible line. On one side, East Side parents and students mill around and talk to one another across bleacher rows. On the other, Boundary parents and students sit in clumps, chatting in small groups. Occasionally, someone glances across the invisible line, their stare filled with heat. But mostly it is as if there is a wall between the two groups.

Gina strides up to the table confidently. "The place is packed," she says proudly. It's as if the fans have come to watch her ref.

Chaos

The horn sounds three times. Malia and Gina go to the benches to shake the coaches' hands and then back to the scorekeepers' table. Gina grabs the ball. "I got this."

Malia nods. The teams cheer. The players walk onto the court as if it's a dark forest. Their eyes dart around, unsure whether to prepare for excitement or danger. They slowly get into position. Gina looks at Malia. She nods, and Gina walks to centre court. She throws the ball into the air. It spins and wobbles, drifting to the right. Both players adjust to the poor throw. The Boundary player reaches the ball first. She taps it to a teammate.

The Boundary players get into their offensive positions. Compared to the first game of the season, the players look like a well-organized army. Each player knows exactly where to go and when.

"Go!" yells the point guard.

The players move, and the point guard passes the ball to her offensive teammate. There is another pass and then another. The East Side players move their feet quickly, hurrying to keep up with the ball. Finally, a Boundary player gets open under the basket. Her teammate passes her the ball and she scores.

In the stands, the Boundary fans cheer loudly. It sounds like a wave is rippling through the gym.

Flo grabs the ball as it goes through the mesh of the hoop and takes it out of bounds. She looks to pass to a teammate, but everyone is guarded closely. Malia watches the Boundary players. They play an aggressive but clean defence. Flo finally manages to inbound the ball to Tilda.

Tilda's defensive player bends her knees and narrows her focus. Tilda takes a dribble toward her. The defensive player takes a single step backward. She gives Tilda no extra space. Rattled by the Boundary player's presence, Tilda pounds the ball on her next dribble. In doing so, she bounces it off her own foot and out of bounds.

Malia blows her whistle. "Boundary ball."

Tilda huffs.

Malia holds the ball out of bounds and waits for the players to get into position. When everyone is ready, she gives the Boundary player the ball and begins to count. Boundary has five seconds to pass the ball inbounds.

One. The Boundary players run around the court. Two. The East Side players stick with their checks. Three. Four.

Just as Malia is about to hit five and blow her whistle to signal that time is up, the complex Boundary play works and a player is wide open under the basket. The inbounder passes her the ball and she scores.

Again Flo gets the ball and sprints to take it out of bounds. She makes a quick pass to Tilda. This time, Tilda's defender is caught off guard. Tilda doesn't hesitate. She dribbles the ball in front of her and sprints down the court. Players from both teams run to get ahead of her. As Tilda nears the basket, she looks up and sees the rim. Boundary Number 16 plants herself between Tilda and the basket. Her feet are set. Her chest is square to Tilda. But Tilda doesn't stop. She jumps into the air to score, crashing into the Boundary player like she's a bowling ball knocking over pins.

Gina blows her whistle. "Block!" she says, exaggerating the blocking gesture. "Boundary Number 16."

"That's right, it is!" says Tilda, hopping to her feet.

"What?!" screams Boundary's coach. "You're terrible!" he yells at Gina.

On the court, several of the Boundary players go to Number 16 to help her up. There are tears in her eyes from being hit so hard. Seeing this, Boundary's coach turns and yells at East Side's coach. "Get your players under control!"

"Get yourself under control!" she yells back.

In the stands, a Boundary parent turns and says something to an East Side parent across the invisible line.

The sounds, sights and emotions envelop Malia's body. It is as if she is wrapped in a blanket made of chaos.

19 TAKING CONTROL

Except for Tilda, who has already marched to the free-throw line to prepare for her shots, the players stand still. The coaches scream at one another. Their voices are drowned out by the yelling fans. Malia glances at the scoreboard. One of the lights flickers, as if it, too, feels the gym's tension. Malia looks to the bleachers, searching desperately for something to ground her. She spots Priya and Carlos. They sit together. Even from a distance, Malia can see the worry on their faces.

Oh my God, thinks Malia suddenly. She narrows her eyes to double check. But nothing changes. Her friends are sitting with the invisible line between them. Each one sits on the opposing side. How did she not notice that before? Malia's pounding heart suddenly feels warm. It's so subtle. She wonders if they did it on purpose, or if it's an accident. Either way, it matters. Even if it's small. It's something.

Malia shakes her head. As if she's come to the surface after being under water, the world returns to her.

Taking Control

She needs to do something. But what? She closes her eyes for a moment and remembers the reffing course. There was nothing in the handbook about rivalries. What would Gloria say? Suddenly, Malia remembers watching Gloria ref the high-school game.

It's not what Gloria would say that matters. It's what she'd do.

Malia blows her whistle, hard. The entire gym stops, stunned by the noise. Malia signals for Gina to join her at centre court. Gina cocks her head to the side as if she might refuse, but then relents.

"What?" she says as she jogs over.

"That was a charge," Malia says.

"It was close."

"No," says Malia firmly. "It wasn't. And you know it."

Gina shrugs. "Maybe, but it doesn't matter now."

"It does matter. Now and later." She points into the stands to the Boundary parent's camera. "The game's being filmed. What do you think Gloria would think of that call?"

"You're going to report me?"

"If you keep making biased calls, then yes. It is our job to be fair. If you can't do your job, then you shouldn't be reffing these games. I'm overturning the call."

"You can't do that," Gina says, floundering. "It'll make me look bad."

"Tough."

"The East Side fans will hate you."

Malia glances toward the players. Poppy holds her arms close to her body, her eyes wide. She bites her bottom lip, as if she's trying to stop it from quivering. "Doesn't matter," says Malia firmly.

She blows her whistle again and walks to the scorekeepers' table. "After talking to my partner, we're changing the call. Charge. Number 12 East Side. Boundary ball on the endline."

As Gina predicted, the East Side fans boo loudly. Malia keeps her back to the stands.

"Come on, Malia!" says East Side's coach.

"Finally, someone does their job," says Boundary's coach.

"You two," says Malia to the coaches. "Come here." Stunned by her tone, they both hesitate. "Now."

The coaches walk to centre court to join her.

"Look at your players," Malia orders. On the court, the girls stand nervously. "Do they look like they're having fun?" She doesn't wait for the coaches to answer. "You both need to . . ." Malia searches for the words. She looks at East Side's coach. Malia realizes a teacher at her school just yelled at her for making the correct call. "You need to act like adults." The coaches' cheeks redden. "Now go back to your benches and coach your teams. And if either of you says anything to one another during play, it will be an automatic technical foul. Am I clear?"

They nod.

Taking Control

Malia grabs the ball and walks purposefully to the end line. The players follow her lead and take their spots on the court. When everyone is ready, Malia hands the ball to the Boundary player. The game begins again.

★★★

After the game, Malia double checks her bag to make sure she's packed everything. She zips it shut and slowly makes her way to the bleachers. The East Side fans wait at the bottom of the stands. They are ready to greet their disappointed daughters, sisters and friends. Malia steadies herself and steps through the crowd, her head up. No one says anything, but they don't glare at her either.

Suddenly, she feels a tug on the right sleeve of her sweatshirt. She turns.

"Hey," says Victor.

"Hi," says Malia shortly. This time, his presence doesn't make her blush. It makes her annoyed.

"We should talk."

"About?"

"You know . . . the party . . . and stuff."

Malia looks around the gymnasium. There are no yelling parents. There are just basketball players and spectators, talking to one another after a big game. "Maybe sometime. But not today. Not for a while."

Before he can respond, Priya has bounced down

the steps. "Vic," she says coldly, nodding at him. She puts herself between Victor and Malia and turns her back to him.

"I didn't know there was such a thing as amazing reffing," says Priya brightly. She leads Malia up the bleachers. "Until today. Now I know."

"Thanks."

"No, seriously," says Priya. "I don't know how you did that. Changing Gina's call at the beginning and then just being in charge. The. Whole. Time."

Carlos greets Malia with a high five. "Good work out there."

Malia nods. Below them, the East Side players walk into the stands to join their parents. To Malia's surprise, Flo walks directly to Malia.

"Thank you, Malia," Flo says seriously.

"What for?"

"For that," she says, gesturing at the court. "By the end, it felt like a normal basketball game." She looks at the score clock and winces. "A basketball game where I was the loser."

"You lost, but you weren't a loser."

"It's true," says Priya. "You played great."

Flo shakes her head. "We lost. I can do better."

"You will," says Malia encouragingly.

"Flo," says one of her teammates. "A bunch of us are going for pizza. You want to come?"

Flo nods and jogs to join her friends.

"Your sister's a competitor," says Priya admiringly.

"Can we get pizza, too?" asks Carlos, looking eager.

"I'm not going near Joey's while my sister's team is there," says Malia.

"We could go to the place in my neighbourhood?"

"Sure," says Malia. "Let's do it." She stops when she sees Priya hesitate. "What's the worst that could happen, Priya?"

"The pizza could be terrible," Priya answers.

"That's perfect. Then we can hold that over Carlos for life," says Malia, nudging Carlos playfully.

As they leave the gym, Malia looks over her shoulder at the court. She thinks about the last two games: one she played, and one she reffed. It's hard to say whether she's prouder of what she did as a player or as a referee. But she knows that, either way, she did what she had to do.